THE CIRCUS OF DR. LAO

CHARLES G. FINNEY

The CIRCUS

of DR. LAO

Vintage Books
A Division of Random House · New York

First Vintage Books Edition, August 1983
Introduction copyright © 1983 by Edward Hoagland
Copyright 1935 by Charles G. Finney
All rights reserved under International and
Pan-American Copyright Conventions. Published in
the United States by Random House, Inc., New
York, and simultaneously in Canada by Random
House of Canada Limited, Toronto. Originally
published by Viking Press, Inc. in 1935. Introduction
originally published by The Limited Editions
Club in 1982.

Library of Congress Cataloging in Publication Data
Finney, Charles G. (Charles Grandison), 1905-
The circus of Dr. Lao.
I. Title.
II. Title: Circus of Doctor Lao.
PS 3511.I64C5 1983   813'.52   83-3486
ISBN 0-394-71617-5

Manufactured in the United States of America

INTRODUCTION

Just as, in a menagerie, some people will pause to marvel before the cage of an exotic creature from another hemisphere, while others haul their children past, scarcely permitting them a glimpse, so, at the circus, some of us gasp at the trapezists' and tumblers' feats, and other paying customers move restlessly in their seats and check their fingernails. In a circus we see mostly what we are ready to see. There is no script but chance and hope and spontaneity, and thus it is appropriate that this masterpiece of circus literature describes an imaginary circus, not a real one. No circus ought to be too 'real.'

Dr. Lao's stupendous show, which arrives abruptly in the Depression town of Abalone, Arizona, one hot August morning, introduces us to a hermaphrodite sphinx, a 2,300-year-old satyr, a lion-lizard-eagle dragon, and a gentle green hound, 'less carnal than a tiger lily,' with chlorophyll in its veins and a plait of ferns for a tail. Also, an angry sea serpent eighty feet long, whose one soft spot is for the circus mermaid; a werewolf that with painful shudders changes itself into an old woman; an ancient, intellectual magician who can bring men back from the dead; and a beautiful medusa who with a glance kills them.

Dr. Lao, the Chinese proprietor, travels with only three wagons and no roustabouts. Yet his numerous tents, black and glossy, stand about like darkened hard-boiled eggs on end. For such miraculous transformations he is indebted to his indispensable thaumaturge, Apollonius, who walks about 'drowned in thought.' Dr. Lao himself is energetic, impulsive, irascible, and resourceful—an impresario who, according to the emergencies of the moment, switches from the language of a poet-professor to the stock-comedy dialect of a Chinese laundryman 'washing the smells out of shirttails,' as two college boys, Slick Bromiezchski and Paul Conrad Gordon, put it to him.

The good doctor does have his troubles. The men in the crowd complain because the werewolf has turned into a woman three hundred years old, not the hot young dish they claim they were promised. A scientist who has examined his fearsome, enigmatic, phlegmatic medusa only wanted to identify the several species of snakes that comprise her hair (for which separate diets must be gathered).

Circuses carry 'a taint of evil or hysteria,' Dr. Lao admits with regret. 'Life sings a song of sex. Sex is the scream of life. . . . Breed, breed, breed. . . . Tumescence and ejaculation.' One cause of his friend Apollonius's melancholy exhaustion is that things on the circus lot are forever getting out of hand—between the sea serpent and the dragon; between Satan and the witches who appear in the finale, some of them too airsick from their flight to perform; between the bear (or is it a 'Russian'?) and the mermaid it carries around the hippodrome; and between the satyr and Miss Agnes Birdsong, a high-school English teacher who had come early to see the 'Pan' that she'd observed driving a wagon during the opening parade through town.

Apollonius of Tyana, who is so old that he was born contemporary with Christ, remains a bit of a perfectionist. He is disappointed when a live turtle that he conjures from a handful of soil for a small boy turns out to have two heads. 'These aren't tricks, madam,' he tells the boy's mother, after calling up 'a big brute' of a flower. 'Tricks are things that fool people. . . . tricks are lies. But these are real flowers, and that was real wine, and that was a real pig. . . . I create; I transpose.'

With enough exertion, and occasionally the aid of a Christian cross, there is nothing he can't accomplish. On his command, Satan stops fornicating with the witches and the satyr obediently pricks balloons with his horns. Out pops Beelzebub from a boar's ear. The witches dance to a chorus of frogs around a fire burning on the carapace of a huge tortoise, who feeds the flames with mouthfuls of dripping peat ripped from the floor of a magical swamp.

Yet what is the point, when the upshot of almost every mythological spectacle endlessly repeats itself in concupiscence and greed; when, in fact, most miracles have an everyday version that attracts no special attention whatsoever?—viz., a tadpole's metamorphosis into a frog. No press agent's hyperbole really equals what goes on at a circus, and no circus extravaganza equals the fish-into-person miracle of a human being.

Furthermore, what's the point for poor Apollonius? The little shriveled dead man whom he brings back to life as a sideshow stunt at Dr. Lao's suggestion has on 'overalls, old worn army shoes with leather laces in them, a blue hickory shirt, and an old worn-out cowboy hat. In the leather sweat band of the hat were the initials "R. K." floridly delineated in indelible pencil.' One of his leather shoe-strings has been broken and retied in several places, the knots looking as if they had been done by a seafaring man, as the author continues to explain with irrepressible exactitude. And Apollonius begins to pray a low, thick prayer. 'His eyeballs turned dead green; thin, hazy stuff floated out of his ears' from the terrific effort of doing so. Finally the man sits up, coughs, asks where he is. 'Well, lemme outa here. I got business to attend to,' he mutters, and rushes off, unaffected by both his own death and his resurrection.

Charles G. Finney, our cheerful author, was only thirty in 1935, when his *Circus* was published, so that his reactions are not the same as those of Apollonius, or even the 'old-like, wealthy-looking party in golf pants' who represents Abalone's solidest citizens. At the time, Finney, great-grandson of a famous Congregational divine who founded Oberlin College, was a veteran of a Missouri country boyhood, a year at the University of Missouri, and three years of garrison duty with Company E, Fifteenth U.S. Infantry Division, in Tientsin, China. An autodidact and intellectual rebel, his favorite twentieth-century writers were Conrad, Kipling, Joyce, Proust, and Anatole France (but included no Americans). He had started the manuscript there in the barracks in the American Compound, writing in longhand, then laid it aside till he got home because it had turned too lecture-y. Later he dedicated the book to an army buddy in Tientsin whom he never crossed paths with again.

China had opened the young soldier's eyes to the breadth of the world, the overpopulation of human beings, the random character of death, the relativity of morality and religion. Still alive in 1983—suffering from Parkinson's disease but after half a century, still living in Tucson—he said in the course of several interviews over the telephone that 'Lao' means 'old' in Mandarin and Cantonese, so 'Dr. Lao' is 'Dr. Old'; that his particular source for the fussy, commonsensical, yet incendiary personality of Dr. Lao was Lao Tehr, the proprietor of a shop which purveyed live Chinese crickets and grasshoppers in straw cages and who had befriended him; that he had discovered Apollonius of Tyana as a mythic figure in Flaubert's *La Tentation de Saint Antoine*; that he never traveled after his trip to China except to go to New York in 1936, when his book achieved a third printing and won the 'Most Original Novel' award of the American Booksellers Association; and that he had been a 'Truman type' of show-me Democrat who voted against Franklin D. Roosevelt all four times. He said his indifference to his literary compatriots extended even to Nathanael West, an almost exact contemporary, whom he resembles as a writer.

However, the book is marked by a brutality more than 'Chinese'—as it would have seemed in the U.S. in 1935. In

slapstick anecdotes, people are 'dobe-walled by Pancho
Villa, and a child is killed by a ricocheting bullet meant
for a deserter. A lady is turned to stone ('carnelian chalcedony') for looking at the medusa. Circuses are brusque
and brutal by nature, anyway—much as they are above
national considerations of patriotism or politics. And this
is a young man's tale, full of cynicism and whimsy, care-
free prurience, elegant language, and gratuitous learning.
Where surreal scenes of violence may be shocking in a
Hollywood novel like West's *Day of the Locust*, which to
some degree speaks to the dilemmas of America as a whole,
a circus lends its air of utter license to any extravagance
of the imagination. Besides, Mr. Finney, after disposing
of the subjects of justice, life, death, and comparative religion so handily, from what seems to have been sheer
exuberance, felt a young man's delight and pride in being
absolutely specific, which is what has kept his writing
fresh. Few 1930s books begin more in the modern manner
than his first paragraph, for instance.

But somehow his failure to travel again, seeking new
fields for his imagination—when travel had proved so in-
valuable to him in the 1920s—signaled, as well, a failure of
ambition. So did the withering of his interest in other
writers of his century. Having no foreknowledge that although he would publish an army memoir and three other
novels during the next fifty years, while writing headlines
and editing the stock-market page at the (Tucson) *Arizona Daily Star*, he would remain essentially a one-book
novelist, Finney announced happily on this, his first dust
jacket that he had been able to find no other job after returning to his homeland than that of part-time proofreader
—which is what 'Mr. Etaoin,' the sanest witness in Abalone, is.

'Etaoin,' another of Mr. Finney's word-games is part
of a phrase by which linotype operators signaled themselves that they had made an error in a given line. We
learn no more of Mr. Etaoin. Just as would be the case in
an earthly circus, each character does a 'turn'; no character

is presented with finality or thoroughness. Not Dr. Lao, who says his preference for luncheon leans more toward sharks' fins than Chinese noodles; not the unicorn, whinnying like a bugle and 'flinging its icicle horn skyward'; nor the satyr, wearing a gold ring in his nose, his torso as lean as a marathon runner's, who eats only vegetables but refuses garlic and onions. (And how bewildered he was, retreating in the early centuries of the A.D. era from the onslaught of Christian celibacy to China, where the footbound maidens could not dance to his piping!)

The dragon eats rattlesnakes, spitting out the rattles, and asphyxiates the desert gnats, snorting smoke and ashes instead of moving its bowels. Yet only its love of the moon enabled the doctor to capture it, by means of a mirror on a mountaintop. The mermaid's sleek-scaled, sea-green fishtail has a fanlike fin on the end as pink as a trout's. Bits of water foam cling to her hair. But the water nymphs have horsey hips and the stomachs of washerwomen.

The seething, glistering sea serpent, with a scarlet throat and a long yellow naked nerve of a tongue the size of a man's arm, vibrates its tail so that 'a whirring arose like a woodsaw's song.' 'Why?' asks young Etaoin, in a duel-like dialogue they engage in in the privacy of the serpent's tent. 'It is my fondest atavism,' the breast replies. He adds that he needs to masturbate nowadays, though he had used to smell his mate all the way across the world and swim to her, stopping at islands along his route to gulp down a coffee-colored boy or girl 'much as you would swallow an oyster and with every bit as much right, if you will pardon an ethical intrusion.' He mocks the proofreader for wearing glasses, although supposedly a member of the Earth's master-race, and later strikes across the big top to seize hold of the doctor during the main performance, only relinquishing him when Apollonius invokes a winter frost to freeze his coils.

Bats 'like wavering, restless flakes of soot'; minks that 'loosened the drawstrings of their scent sacs'; scorpions, worms, Gila monsters, salamanders in a muddy pig wallow

—seldom since Christopher Smart has a writer so cele-
brated the dukes and troopers of the animal kingdom, as
well as its fishiness, pigginess, snakiness. A gigantic roc's
egg hatches. 'Silly pinfeathers, big as ostrich plumes,
adorned its grey skin, and the yellow at the corners of its
mouth was as yellow as butter. . . . The roc chick stood
weeping in the litter of eggshell. It opened its mouth and
wailed with horrible hunger.'

This verisimilitude to the misery of birth is too strong
for the customers, however. And one father had told his
kids that the egg was a fake, so after watching it hatch,
they have to leave. The mermaid, with whom Dr. Lao himself is in love, provokes only the question, 'What do you
feed her, doc?' When a local widow, Mrs. Howard T.
Cassan, in her thin brown dress and low shoes, comes to
consult Apollonius as fortuneteller, he speaks for our impatient author:

'Tomorrow will be like today. . . . You will think no
new thoughts. You will experience no new passions. Older
you will become but not wiser. Stiffer but not more dignified. Childless you are, and childless you shall remain.
Of that suppleness . . . , of that strange simplicity which
once attracted a few men to you, neither endures. . . . Must
I tell you how many times you will become annoyed at
the weather . . . ? Shall I compute the pounds of pennies
you will save shopping at bargain center ?' he asks harshly
—throwing in the terrible thought that she has a voice in
government and that enough people voting the way she
does could change the face of the world. But her only re-
sponse is to ask Apollonius to move in with her.

Mr. Finney's sympathy for humdrum people and ordinary lives had a short fuse. Perhaps partly as a result, his
book finally ran out of steam. When the delight and spontaneity begin to wane, we know the performance is almost
over—not because of some inner novelistic logic, but because, just as at a circus, the acts that he has brought to
town have now all appeared and it is simply *over*. In fact,

the book's shortness probably explains why it is not better known, compared to bulkier underground classics, and why it needs reviving.

At the end, 'a thin wispy rain came weeping.' Also at the end is the funniest section, and Mr. Finney's own favorite, the Catalogue, wherein he sums up everything and everyone who has pranced by. There are ticks, camels, polar bears, crustaceans, frigate birds, geologists, silly people's silly wives.

Wonders were what interested Finney—'real honest-to-goodness freaks that had been born of hysterical brains rather than diseased wombs'—'the sports, the offthrows . . . of the lust of the spheres,' foaled from the Earth, suggests the good doctor, the way the Surinam toad bears its offspring, through the skin of its back. Dr. Lao's perpetual, exasperated dither, the lassitude and boredom of Apollonius, and the pell-mell terror of much of the show, are the price of having a performance at all—which, for reasons unstated, of course must go on.

Always the point is indicated that the natural wonders next door—a child's somersault, the birth of a kitten—are equal to what is seen here. A circus works its marvels by parading in front of us what we could see anyhow if we were more alert and less prejudiced, more curious and devout, and opened our eyes.

For, 'This is the circus of Dr. Lao' (as that personage explains, banging a gong) . . .

'Oh, we've spared no pains and we've spared no dough;
And we've dug at the secrets of long ago;
And we've risen to Heaven and plunged Below,
For we wanted to make it one hell of a show. . . .
Long past the time when the winter snow
Has frozen the summer's furbelow.'

EDWARD HOAGLAND

THE CIRCUS OF DR. LAO

In the *Abalone* (Arizona) *Morning Tribune* for August third there appeared on page five an advertisement eight columns wide and twenty-one inches long. In type faces grading from small pica to ninety-six point the advertisement told of a circus to be held in Abalone that day, the tents to be spread upon a vacant field on the banks of the Santa Ana River, a bald spot in the city's growth surrounded by all manner of houses and habitations.

Floridly worded, the advertisement made claims which even Phineas Taylor Barnum might have hedged at advancing. It alleged for the show's female personnel a pulchritude impossible to equal in any golden age of beauty or physical culture. The mind of man could not conceive of women more beautiful than were the charmers of this circus. Though the whole race of man were bred for feminine beauty as the whole race of Jersey cattle is bred for butterfat, even then lovelier women could not be produced than the ones who graced this show. . . . Nay, these were the most beautiful women of the world; the whole world, not just the world of today, but the world since time began and the world as long as time shall run.

Nor were the wild animals on display at the circus any less sensational than were the girls. Not elephants or tigers or hyenas or monkeys or polar bears or hippopotami; anyone and everyone had seen such as those time after time. The sight of an African lion was as banal today as that of an airplane. But here were animals no man had ever seen before; beasts fierce beyond all dreams of ferocity;

1

serpents cunning beyond all comprehension of guile; hybrids strange beyond all nightmares of fantasy.

Furthermore, the midway of the circus was replete with sideshows wherein were curious beings of the netherworld on display, macabre trophies of ancient conquests, resurrected supermen of antiquity. No glass-blowers, cigarette fiends, or frogboys, but real honest-to-goodness freaks that had been born of hysterical brains rather than diseased wombs.

Likewise, the midway would house a fortuneteller. Not an ungrammatical gypsy, not a fat blonde mumbling silly things about dark men in your life, not a turbaned mystic canting of the constellations; no, this fortuneteller would not even be visible to you, much less take your hand and voice generalities concerning your life lines. Anonymous behind the veil of his mystery he would speak to you and tell you of foreordained things which would come into your life as the years unfolded. And you were warned not to enter his tent unless you truly wanted to know the truth about your future, for never under any conditions did he lie about what was going to happen; nor was it possible for you after learning your future to avert in any way its unpleasant features. He absolutely would not, however, forecast anything of an international or political nature. He was perfectly capable of so doing, of course, but the management had found that such prophecies, inasmuch as they were invariably true, had in the past been used to unfair and dishonorable advantage by unscrupulous financiers and politicians: that which had been meant for mankind had been converted to personal gain—which was not ethical.

And for men only there was a peepshow. It was educational rather than pornographic. It held no promise of hermaphroditic goats or randy pony stallions lusting after women. Nor any rubberstamp striptease act. But out of the erotic dramas and dreams of long-dead times had been culled a figure here, an episode there, a fugitive vision elsewhere, all of which in combination produced an effect that no ordinary man for a long series of days would forget or, for that matter, care to remember too vividly. Because of the unique character of this segment of the circus, attendance would be limited to men over twenty-one, married men preferred; and absolutely no admittance to any man under the influence of liquor.

In the main tent the circus performance proper, itself diverting beyond description with colorful acts and remarkable scenes, would end with a formidable spectacle. Before your eyes would be erected the long-dead city of Woldercan and the terrible temple of its fearful god Yottle. And before your eyes the ceremony of the living sacrifice to Yottle would be enacted: a virgin would be sanctified and slain to propitiate this deity who had endured before Bel-Marduk even, and was the first and mightiest and least forgiving of all the gods. Eleven thousand people would take part in the spectacle, all of them dressed in the garb of ancient Woldercan. Yottle himself would appear, while his worshipers sang the music of the spheres. Thunder and lightning would attend the ceremonies, and possibly a slight earthquake would be felt. All in all it was the most tremendous thing ever to be staged under canvas.

Admission 10c to the circus grounds proper. 25c admission to the big top; children in arms free. 10c admission to the sideshows. 50c admission to the peepshow. Parade at 11 A.M. Midway open at 2 P.M. Main show starts at 2:45. Evening performance at 8. Come one, come all. The greatest show on earth.

The first person to notice anything queer about the ad, aside from its outrageous claims, was the proofreader of the *Tribune* checking it for typographical errata the night before it appeared in the paper. An ad was an ad to Mr. Etaoin, the proofreader, a mass of words to be examined for possible error both of omission and commission, manner and matter. And his meticulous, astigmatic, spectacle-bolstered eyes danced over the type of this full-page advertisement, stopping at the discovery of transposition or mis-spelling long enough for his pencil to indicate the trouble on the margin of the proof, then dancing on through the groups of words to the end. After he had read the ad through and corrected what needed correcting, he held it up at arm's length to read over the bigger type again and ascertain whether he had missed anything at the first perusal. And looking at the thing in perspective that way, he discovered that it was anonymous, that it carried on endlessly as to the wonders of the show, but never said whose show it was, that never a name appeared anywhere in all that overabundance of description.

"Something's screwy," reflected Mr. Etaoin. And he took the ad copy to the *Tribune* advertising manager for counsel and advice.

"Look here," he said to that gentleman, "here's a whole page of hooey about some circus and not a word as to whose circus it is. Is that O.K.? Is that the way it's supposed to run in the paper? Generally these circus impresarios are hell on having their names smeared all over the place."

"Let's see," said the ad manager, taking up the copy. "By God, that is funny. Who sold this ad, anyway?"

"Steele's name's on the ticket," offered the proofreader. Advertising Solicitor Steele was summoned.

"Look here," said the ad manager, "there aint any name or nothing on this ad. What about that?"

"Well, sir, I don't know," said Steele vaguely. "A little old Chinaman brought the copy in to me this morning, paid cash for the ad, and said it was to run just exactly the way it was written. He said we could use our judgment about the type face and so on, but the words must be exactly the way he had 'em. I told him O.K. and took the money and the ad, and that's all I know about it. I guess that's the way he wants it, though. He was so insistent we mustn't change anything."

"Yeah, but doesn't he want his name in there somewhere?" persisted the proofreader.

"Damn if I know," said Steele.

"Let it ride just the way it is," ruled the manager. "We got the money. That's the main thing in any business."

"Sure must be some show," said the proofreader. "Did you guys read this junk?"

"Nah, I didn't read it," said Steele.

"I aint read an ad in ten years," said the manager. "I just look at 'em kinda; I don't read 'em."

"O.K.," said Mr. Etaoin, "she goes as is then. You're the boss."

The next person to notice something unusual in the page display was Miss Agnes Birdsong, high-school English teacher. Two words in it bothered her: pornographic and hermaphroditic. She knew what pornography meant, having looked it up after reading a review of Mr. Cabell's *Jurgen.* But hermaphroditic had her at a loss. She thought she suspected she knew what it meant; she detected the shadows of the god and the goddess, but their adjectival marriage left her bewildered. She pondered a little, then reached for her dictionary. A guardian of the language could do no less. The definitions left her wiser but not sadder. She returned to the ad to wonder further what a fugitive vision seen through a peephole would be like. She pondered upon the conjuring up in a stuffy circus tent of an erotic dream of a long-dead day. She wished momentarily she were a man. She thought, and quickly slew the thought, of dressing up like a man and attending that peep-show. "I'll go and see the parade," compromised Miss Agnes Birdsong.

The children of Plumber Rogers saw the ad while they were searching for the comics. It was a tremendous occasion. A circus in town that very day and they hadn't even known it was coming. A parade in two hours that would pass two blocks from the Rogers house. Clowns. Elephants. Tigers. Calliopes. Bands. Horses. Fanfare and pomp. The yellow glare of Abalone took on a golden glow for the children of Plumber Rogers, for a circus was in town.

"Now, don't go getting all excited, you kids," said the plumber uneasily. "I don't know whether you'll get to go or not." (He hadn't had work since the first day of the depression.) "I don't think it'll be much of a circus anyway."

He took the paper from them and read the ad for himself. . . . Eleven thousand people would take part in the spectacle . . . "Why, that's a goddam lie!" said Plumber Rogers. "There aint hardly that many people in Abalone."

"Oh, John," said Mrs. Rogers, shocked; "you oughtn't to talk that way before the children."

But John wasn't listening. He was reading about the women in the circus.

"Tell you what; let's go, Sarah," he said. "The kids haven't seen anything for a long time. Maybe something'll turn up in the way of work pretty soon. These hard times can't last much longer."

At nine o'clock the chief of police read the advertisement. He turned to the desk sergeant. "Say, I didn't know there was going to be a circus in town today. Did you know anything about it?"

"Naw," said the sergeant. "I don't pay no 'tention to circuses anyway. I aint been to one since I was a kid. Never did like the damn things a whole hell of a lot anyway."

The chief phoned the city clerk's office. "Say, about this circus that's advertised in the paper this morning. I didn't know nothing about it till just now I read about it. They got a permit, do you know?"

He listened awhile. "Yeah . . . yeah . . . no . . . I guess so . . . I don't know . . . yeah . . . no . . . oh, sure . . . yeah . . . yeah . . . no . . . uh huh. Good-by."

"Well?" said the desk sergeant.

"The clerk claims an old Chink came in and got a permit for a circus just before quitting time last night. Said the Chink had the owner's written consent to use the vacant lot for the show."

"Well?" said the desk sergeant.

"Well, you send a couple of guys out there this afternoon to look the joint over," said the chief. "I guess it's all right, but it seems kind of screwy to me anyway. Did you ever hear of a Chink running a circus before?"

"Aw, I aint paid no 'tention to circuses since I was a kid," said the desk sergeant.

A traffic officer of the railroad read the ad at seven-thirty while he was eating breakfast just before going to work. Behind one of his ears a pimple loomed temptingly, ripe for a squeezing. His hair was dryish and thinnish and untidy and brownish and needed further combing. His flesh was the flesh of one neither young nor old, but more old than young, more repulsive than tempting. Cannibals might have eaten him; shipwrecked mariners never. An undiscerning woman might have loved him; a cinema queen never. He wasn't a very good traffic officer; he might have made a failure of the insurance business. Heaven perhaps could comfort him; this world never. His two young sons sometimes would wonder how his hands would look in handcuffs, his feet in ballet slippers, his nose in a stein of beer. He read the ad uneasily, remarking to his wife petulantly:

"Here's a damn circus in town. But it never came over the railroad; must have its own trucks. Just some more business we didn't get. By George, there's lots of it we don't get any more. First thing I know they won't be needing traffic men on the line any more. Then what in hell'll we do?"

"Oh, now, don't start worrying," said his wife, "till you've got something to worry about."

A state quarantine inspector came in from his nightly vigil at the bug station out on the California highway and at breakfast in a restaurant met a fellow-inspector from the bug station on the New Mexico highway. They saw the ad in the restaurant paper.

"Did you see any circus come by your place last night?" asked Inspector Number One.

"Nope," said Inspector Number Two.

"Neither did I. It must have come in over the railroad,

8 The Circus of Dr. Lao

I guess. If you aint got nothing to do this afternoon, let's go to the damn thing."

"Awright," said Inspector Number Two. "I kinda like the goddam things."

A lawyer who prided himself on his knowledge of history and religion read the ad and bogged down at the "long-dead city of Woldercan" and the "fearful god Yottle." He went to his encyclopædia to refresh his memory. Neither city nor deity could he find. He wasn't sure about Bel-Marduk either, so he looked him up, too. Bel, however, was there. "Yottle . . ." thought the lawyer, "Woldercan . . . baloney; somebody's been making up a lot of stuff. Fooling the people all of the time. Wonder what a circus conception of a god previous to Bel-Marduk would be like. Oh, Lord, what'll people think of next? Believe I'll go to the darn thing. Can't do any worse than bore me to death."

A widow, a Mrs. Howard T. Cassan, read the advertisement at quarter of ten. ". . . the midway will house a fortuneteller . . . veiled in mystery . . . prophecies invariably true . . ." Mrs. Cassan always went to fortunetellers. When none was available she cast the cards or séanced with ouija. She had had her future foretold so many times that in order to fulfill all the forecasts she would have to live ninety-seven more years and encounter and charm a war-strength regiment of tall, dark men. "I'll go and ask this man—let's see—yes, I'll ask him about that oil well I dreamed about," said Mrs. Howard T. Cassan.

Two college youths from back East, Slick Bromiezchski and Paul Conrad Gordon, at the moment in Abalone, Arizona, after an outing in old Mexico, read the ad and decided to see the circus.

"Let's take in that peepshow," said Slick.

"You're damn right; and we'll take it in cockeyed drunk, too," said Paul. "Refusing admittance to men under the influence of liquor is a challenge no Sigma Omicron Beta can overlook."

Mr. Etaoin, the *Tribune* proofreader, conned the ad again at his breakfast at ten-thirty to see if he had overlooked any errors in it the night before. Finding none pleased him. He regarded the page fondly, marking the emphasis gained by the use of white space around the big black type, commending the restrained use of italics, admiring the thin Goudy caps and small caps. The sense of what he looked at piqued him. "Wonder what kind of show it is?" thought Mr. Etaoin. "Believe I'll go to the thing."

Mr. Larry Kamper read the ad cursorily in a cast-aside *Tribune* as he lounged under the palm trees in the park by the railroad station waiting for a freight train to leave Abalone. Larry knew not what train he was waiting for, nor in which direction it might be going, nor where he would get off. But he didn't mind. He had recently been discharged from the army, still had a little money, was reasonably his own master and comparatively free from worry. His last permanent address had been Company E, 15th U.S. Infantry, American Compound, Tientsin, China. He had been discharged at Fort Mason after his return to America on an army transport, had been paid all that was due him, and now was touring the great Southwest, a land hitherto out of his ken, on sidedoor Pullmans. So he lounged under the palm trees in the park near the railroad station, waiting for a freight train to go in either one direction or another, and cursorily read the ad in the cast-aside *Tribune*. And, lo, upon the world-weary traveler there fell a pall of nostalgia, and waveringly a ghost cry from the bones of his dead youth smote his ears: he had not seen a circus for ten years; to be a little boy again; to tremble at the sight of strange animals; to recapture the simple thrill of wonderment: that would be pleasure; that would be good. Larry the infantryman, Larry the booze-fighter, Larry the whorechaser, Larry the loudmouthed, read the ad and longed for his boyhood. And presently he got to his feet and wondered what time it was and started for the circus grounds.

Six blocks down Main Street Larry Kamper encountered the parade. Realizing he was too early for the show, he shouldered his way through the mass of Mexicans that cluttered the curb to get a look at the procession.

He almost laughed when he saw it. Only three frowzy little beast-drawn wagons, the first driven by an old Chinaman, the second by a pale bearded man, the last by a Jewish-looking fellow with a cap of goat horns on his head. There was a big coiled grey snake in the Chinaman's wagon, a bear in the second wagon, a green dog in the last.

"Hey," said a man standing beside Larry, "what sort of animal is that thing pulling the first cart there?"

Larry looked and saw a horse bearing on its forehead a long thin white horn.

"Just some fake," said Larry. "What d'you call them things? Singlehorns? That aint it. Monohorns? Naw . . . uh . . . unicorns? That's it. Unicorn. Fellah took a horse and made a unicorn out of it by pasting a horn on its head, I guess."

"Yah, but that aint no horse like any ever what I see," said the man. "Look at thet there tail. Ever see a horse with a tail like that critter's got?"

"Well, I don't know a hell of a lot about horses," said Larry. "I been in the infantry six years. But it aint no unicorn; I know that, 'cause there aint no unicorns, nor ever was."

"Well, sir, that thing aint a horse either," said the man. "I been boy-raised with horses, and I can tell 'em when I see 'em; and that aint no horse."

"I guess it's a freak of some kind then," said Larry. And he also said: "Well, Jeesis, what's that thing driving the last wagon?"

The man looked and said: "Why, it's just a feller with some goat horns on his head. Another fake, I reckon."

"I never seen a man like that before," said Larry. "Look at his feet."

"What's the matter with his feet?"

"Aw, he pulled 'em down too quick. He had 'em up on the dashboard for just a second. Had awful funny-looking shoes on, if you could call 'em shoes. Look at his face, ever see a face like that before?"

"Sure," said the man; "hell of a lot of 'em. What's wrong with his face?"

"I dunno," said Larry. "The whole thing's screwy, anyway. Circus parade with only three wagons! My Gawd. Hey, what's that animal in the last wagon?"

"You got me, brother. Looks like a dog, though."

"That aint no dog," said Larry.

"Well, say now, let's get together on some of this stuff," protested the man. "Which of us is cockeyed, anyway?"

"Oh, to hell with the parade," said Larry. "I got some money. Come on, let's get a glass of beer."

"Right," said the man.

They went into Harry Martinez's place.

"Two cervezas," said the man to Barkeep Harry.

"Naw, naw," said Larry. "I just want beer."

"That means beer out here; it's Spanish," grinned Harry. Larry was relieved. "Awright, then. What'dya think of the parade?"

"I didn't think a hell of a lot of it," said Harry, " 'cept that I couldn't figure why they had that man in the second cage. What was he, a wild man from Borneo or something?"

"Man?" said Larry's companion. "I didn't see no man in a cage. There was a snake and a bear and something what looked like a dog kinda, but I didn't see no man. Did you?" he asked Larry.

"I dunno what the hell I saw now," said Larry.

"Well," said Harry Martinez, "I'm here to tell you that I got good eyes, an' that in the cage on the second wagon of that there parade I seen a man. He looked like a Russian or something. And what kind of an animal was that what was pulling that second wagon; tell me that, either of you."

"I didn't rightly notice," said Larry's companion.

"Neither did I," said Larry.

"Well," said Harry Martinez, "I did. Did you ever hear of a sphinx?"

"That big statue thing in Arabia?"

"Yeah. Well, it looked like a sphinx pulling that second wagon. 'Course it was a fake. Big mule, I reckon, tricked out in a lion's hide."

"Nope," said Larry, "I remember now. That wasn't no mule."

"Well, what the hell was it then?" asked his friend.

"I dunno, but it wasn't a mule, that's a cinch," said Larry, finishing his beer.

"Two more beers," said his friend.

"Right," said Harry Martinez.

Mr. Etaoin, the *Tribune* proofreader, stepped out of the restaurant onto Main Street and saw the parade coming his way. He lit a cigarette and awaited its coming.

When it came, he gazed at it bemusedly wondering if he saw aright. An elderly lady tapped his arm. She had a little boy with her.

"Please, mister, can you tell us what kind of a snake that is in the wagon? Is it something they caught here in Arizona? We're just out from the East, you know, and don't know all the animals here yet."

Mr. Etaoin regarded the reptile in the slow-moving wagon. It had no scales; only a grey slimy hide like a catfish.

"I don't know what it is, lady," he said; "but it's not an Arizona snake, that's certain. They don't get that big out here. Matter of fact, I don't know where in the world snakes do get as big as that fellow is."

"Maybe it's a sea serpent, grandma," said the little boy.

"That's as good an idea as any," agreed Mr. Etaoin.

Two business men came alongside. "Lord, but that's a big snake," said one. "Wonder what kind it is?"

"It's a sea serpent," said the little boy.

"It is, huh?" said the man. "Well, by George, I always heard of them things; kinda like myths, you know. But this is the first time I ever really saw one. So that's the sea serpent, huh? Well, sir, he's a monster; I'll give him credit for that. Yessir."

The man with him said: "What's that man doing in the second cage?"

"That's no man, Bill; that's a bear. What's wrong with your eyes?"

"Looks like a man to me," said Bill. "What do you call it, friend?" he asked Mr. Etaoin.

"My glasses are kinda dusty," said the proofreader, "but it looks to me like a man that walks like a bear."

"Well, I say it's a bear what walks like a man," said the first business man facetiously. "Man that walks like a bear . . . haw, haw. That's pretty good! Where's he going to walk to in that cage? Huh?"

"Why, it's a Russian, isn't it?" asked the old lady.

"Good Lord, woman," said Bill, "we aint that bad yet here in Arizona. We don't pen Russians up and put 'em on display with animals; that is, not yet we don't."

"Here, now," said the first man to Bill; "don't talk to a lady that way. You said it was a man yourself, didn't you? What difference does it make whether it's a Russian or not? You got to excuse him, lady."

"I don't give a damn whether it's a Russian or an Eskimo or a Democrat!" said Bill. "By God, it aint no bear, and that's that."

"Well, I never heard such language in all my life!" announced the old lady. "If that's western chivalry for you, the sooner I get back to Sedalia the better!"

Mr. Etaoin, to make conversation, said: "What kind of a donkey is it pulling the last wagon?"

"Why, it's just a common ordinary everyday good-for-nothing lousy lowdown jackass of a donkey," said Bill truculently. "I aint going to get in no argument about him, fellah. I'm sorry, lady, for speaking the way I did. I don't feel so good this morning."

The little boy piped up: "It's a burro, isn't it, mister?"

"Have it your own way, lad. I don't care if it's a walrus."

"How come it's so doggone yellow?" asked the first man.

"It looks like it was made of gold," said the old lady brightly.

Bill started to laugh. "Haw, haw, haw! The golden ass! The golden ass!"

Bill's companion took his arm. "Come on, Bill; let's go. Folks are beginning to look at you funny."

"Are people all like that in Abalone?" the old lady asked Mr. Etaoin.

"No, not all of 'em," he apologized. "Just one or two now and then."

The two college youths from back East came out of their hotel and climbed into their old touring car; Slick Bromiezchski driving, Paul Conrad Gordon giving advice: "Choke it, boy; choke hell out of it."

The car started and they got as far as Main Street when a red light halted them. Then the parade came along and halted them some more.

"There's the circus," said Slick. "Where's the peepshow float?"

"Patience," said Paul Conrad. "They don't put their peepshows on parade. This is only the teaser to the main dish."

"Sure is a hell of a parade," said Slick. "Old Chink with one foot in the grave; Christlike looking personage; and that guy made up to look like Rodin's Faun—or am I thinking of Praxiteles? Anyhow, what do you think of it, Oom Powl?"

"Rodin's Faun!" said Paul; "that's what I was trying to think of. Afternoon of a faun. Nymphs. You know."

"Sure. But why that particular stream of consciousness?"

"It's the guy with the horns on his head," said Paul. "Suppose he were real?"

"All right. I'm supposing as hard as I can. Now what?"

"Well, good Lord, can you imagine a real honest-to-god satyr driving a gold-plated mule down the main drag of a hick town?"

"Sure. I can imagine anything. What of it?"

"Oh, nothing. Let's go. Time's flying. We got to get under the influence and make a test case on the circus grounds, you will recall."

On her way to the Cash and Carry, Mrs. Howard T. Cassan was momentarily held up by the parade.

"My, what horrid animals," she thought. "I wonder which one is the fortuneteller—which one of the men, that is."

From a window in an upper apartment over her head a female voice called down: "Excuse me, please, but can you tell from where you are whether that's a man or a bear in the second wagon?"

"Why, it's a bear, I believe," Mrs. Cassan called back obligingly. "Though I don't know what kind of a bear."

"The lady on the corner says it's a bear, Joe," said the voice.

"Bear, hell," said Joe's voice. "Don't you think I know a Russian when I see one?"

"Well, dear me!" said Mrs. Cassan.

The lawyer who prided himself on his extra-legal knowledge watched the parade tolerantly from his kitchen door with his wife.

"It's sort of pitiful, isn't it?" he said. "A goofy little road show like that hanging silly disguises on animals to make them look like things out of mythology. It isn't even well done. That horse rigged up like a sphinx, for instance. Look at the fool woman's face on the thing. You can tell from here it's paper mâché or something. And those absurd breasts hanging down in front of it."

"Now, Frank," said his wife, "don't be vulgar, please. What's that man doing in that cage, do you suppose? Is he some sort of a freak?"

"Why, that's not a man, honey; that's a bear. Looks like a big grizzly from here."

His wife pretended to smell his breath. "What have you been drinking, Frank, dear? Don't you credit me with enough intelligence to distinguish a man from a bear?"

Frank looked at her in mock alarm. "I told you last week you ought to get fitted for glasses, honey. I'm going to take you down myself right after lunch and have the doctor fix you up with a triple-strong pair of lenses. A man; haw, haw, haw!"

His wife got sore. "You make me so damn mad when you sneer that way. I mean when you laugh that sneering way. You do it on purpose. You know good and well that's a man; you're just trying to be funny."

The lawyer looked at his wife strangely. "All right, honey," he said quietly; "it's a man. Come on; let's go in and eat."

The telephone rang as they were sitting down. Frank answered it:

"Hello."

" 'Lo, Frank?"

"Yeah."

"This is Harvey. Did you folks see the parade go by just now?"

"Yeah."

"Well, so did Helen and I. We couldn't decide what that was in the middle cage. Did you notice? We been having quite an argument, and I thought I'd call you up to settle it. Helen claimed it was a bear in there, but I thought it was a Russian. What did you folks make it out to be?"

"We're undecided, too," said Frank and hung up.

Quarantine Inspector Number Two saw the parade as he leaned out his coupé window to yell at Inspector Number One, who was ambling toward him down Main Street. Inspector Number One got in the coupé and watched with him.

"Man, that sure is a big snake," he said. "Reminds me of that big sidewinder I killed down on the Beeswax road last spring. Thing had sixteen rattles."

"Must've been sixteen years old then, " said Inspector Number Two.

"Oh, that's the way you tell, is it? I always figured it was something like that. What do you make of that bear there? Is he a Sonoran grizzly?"

"I don't see no bear."

"Well, it's right there in that second wagon, bigger'n hell."

"You're still asleep, fellah; that's a man. Looks like a Russian."

"Yeah? Who is it, Trotsky?"

"I dunno who it is, but it aint no bear. Say, look at that dog, will you! Ever see a green dog before?"

"There's lots of things in that parade I aint never seen before. Just how in hell do you figure that aint a bear in the middle wagon?"

" 'Cause I seen bears and I seen men; and I can tell a man from a bear as far as I can see either of 'em; and that thing is a man and not a bear; and I'm tired of arguing about anything so damn foolish."

"All right," said Inspector Number One. "Don't go getting hard about it. I aint going to argue with you. What do you make of the dog?"

"Well, it's jest about the biggest dog I ever seen, but I never seen one that color before. Look at its hide; the thing shore has rough hair. Good Lord, its teeth are green, too. Well, what kind of a dog is that, anyway?"

"You got me. That's a nice little burro pulling the last cart."

"That aint no burro."

"Well, what the hell is it, then; an elephant?"

"Say, what's the matter with you today? You know that aint no burro. You know burros've got hair on 'em. You know burros aint slick like they was made of glass like that thing is. You know they don't shine that way."

"Well, it looks like a burro."

"Yeah. You thought that man looked like a bear, too. I don't know what's got into you today."

"By God, that was a bear! You better pull yourself together, guy. They got a booby hatch in this state for people what gets funny notions." Inspector Number One got out of the coupé. "Don't go getting any funny notions when you're on shift tonight, or somebody's liable to get your job. I'm telling you straight, see?"

Inspector Number Two lit a cigar. A policeman friend of his came up and jocularly cautioned him about parking too long in one spot."

"Listen, Tom," said the inspector, "did you see that parade go by just now?"

"Yeah, I saw the crazy thing. Hell of a big bear they had in one of the wagons."

"Oh, Lord!" said the inspector and drove away.

The railroad traffic officer's wife called him up at about eleven o'clock.

"Ed," she said, "have you seen the circus parade? The children want to go over and watch it, but it's so far from the house I'm sort of afraid to let them. Is it really worth watching, do you know?"

"Yes, I just now saw it," said Ed. "All they got is three wagons pulled by horses or something. I thought sure there'd be some trucks. I can't imagine how they got into town. I know those beasts didn't pull those wagons all the way from California or from wherever they came. No, the kids wouldn't like it, I don't believe. There's a big snake in one wagon and a wild man or something in the other and a funny-looking dog in the last. I don't think the kids would like it, really. No clowns or anything like that."

One of his fellow-workers, listening in on the conversation, said: "Where was that wild man, Ed? I must have missed him."

"In the middle wagon."

"Ho, ho, ho! That wasn't no wild man; that was a big

bear. Funny thing: a couple of guys out in front made the same mistake you did. Thought the bear was a man. Haw, haw, haw!"

"Well, it surer'n hell looked like a man," said Ed.

"You been worrying about that circus so much all morning," said the desk sergeant to the chief of police; "there goes the parade now—why don't you go out and look at it?"

Its inertia broken by these pregnant words, practically the entire force left off lounging around the spittoons and went out on the curb by the parked Black Maria to watch the little procession go by. The old Chinaman driving the first wagon noted the uniforms and bowed to vested authority. The unicorn harnessed between the shafts noted the brass buttons, too, and flinging its icicle horn skyward, whinnied like a bugle and danced on its hind feet. The aged Chinaman flailed it with his lash, and its caperings subsided.

"That's a high-stepping bronc he's got hooked on there," commented one of the lesser policemen. "How'd it get that horn, d'yuh reckon? Never heard of a horse having a horn before."

"That aint no horse," said another policeman; "that's a unicorn."

"What's a unicorn?"

"Why, it's something like a cross between a horse and a rhino, I guess. They come from Armenia, I believe, or some goddam place like that."

"Oh, sure, I remember reading about them in school now when I was a kid. Aint they awfully rare or something?"

"Yep. Rarer than hell."

"Man, that's a big snake in there. Wonder what it is."

"Looks like a boa constrictor to me."

"Nope," said one of the motorcycle patrolmen, "it aint a boa constrictor. It's an anaconda from South America. Teddy Roosevelt caught one when he was hunting down there years ago."

"Is it poisonous?"

"Oh, sure. That thing's got enough poison to kill a whole regiment."

"Jesus! Sure is some snake!"

"I've seen 'em bigger'n that one when the liquor's in me," said a big fat cop.

The other officers laughed and agreed.

The desk sergeant, who had been watching from the window, called out: "Hey, chief, we ought to have a wagon like that middle one there to pen up drunks in like that feller's penned up."

"Yeah," said the chief, "it's a good idea; only what feller you talking about?"

"The one in the wagon."

The chief chuckled. "Heh, heh. Old Baldy thinks that bear is a man. Guess his sight's failing."

"I don't see no bear, chief," said the motorcycle patrolman.

"Well, it's right in front of your goddam nose. Wipe off your goggles and you can see it."

"I'll be damned if that's a bear," persisted the patrolman.

"Well," said the chief in disgust, "there's two people I don't ever argue with: one's a woman and the other's a damn fool. And you aint no woman!"

Mrs. Rogers asked her three children if they had enjoyed the parade.

"Naw," said Willie. "There wasn't no clowns there, ner elephants, ner nuthin'."

"Well, I liked it," said Alice. "There was the prettiest little mule. All shiny like it was gold or something."

"I liked the big green dog," said little Edna.

"A green dog?" said Mrs. Rogers. "Now, Edna, what are you saying?"

"Well, it was green, mother. Just as green as grass. Only it didn't never bark or anything."

"And then there was that thing like that statue on the table," said Willie.

"What statue?" asked Mrs. Rogers.

Willie brought the statue in. "This one. What's the name of it, mother?"

"Well, it's called a sphinx, but I'm quite sure you didn't see a sphinx in a circus parade."

"Yes we did, mother," said Alice, "a real live sphinx. It looked like a woman sticking her front out of a lion. It was pulling a wagon with a big bear in it."

"It wasn't a bear," said Edna, "it was a man."

"It was a bear," said Alice.

"It was a man."

"It was a bear."

"It was a man."

"Oh, heavens! Don't start that now," said Mrs. Rogers. "What was it, Willie, a bear or a man?"

"I thought it was a Russian," said Willie.

Mrs. Rogers sat down. "You children see the strangest things sometimes. What else was there, Alice?"

"Well, there was a man with horns on his head like a goat; and there was a Chinaman; and there was a snake; and there was a man what looked like God."

"Oh, Alice," said Mrs. Rogers, "how can you say such a thing?"

"Well," said Alice, "he looked just like those pictures of Jesus in the Sunday-School book, didn't he, Edna?"

"Just exactly," said Edna. "Long brown hair and beard and white robes and everything. He looked awfully old, though."

"Well, was that all there was in the parade?" asked Mrs. Rogers.

"That's all, mother. There weren't any clowns or elephants or bands or camels or anything."

"Weren't there any horses?"

"There was a horse with a horn on its head, but it had a funny tail," said Edna.

"Well, it must have been a queer parade," said Mrs. Rogers. "I wish I had seen it."

A little later Mr. Rogers came in with a funny look on his face.

"What's the matter?" his wife asked.

"I dunno," said the plumber; "it don't seem right. That parade I saw just now. Oh, yeah, before I forget; I got work, Sarah, nine months' work starting tomorrow."

"Well, thank God!" said Mrs. Rogers. "Where? Tell me quick!"

"Oh, maintenance stuff down at the hotel. But I wanted to tell you about that parade. Never saw such a thing. Got a snake there I bet's eighty feet long if he's an inch. And then there was a Chink. Funny old bird. Oh, yeah; but what I wanted to tell you about was a bear they had in a cage. There was a fellah standing beside me tried to tell me it was a man. Ever hear of such a thing? Couldn't tell a bear from a man! I thought he was joking at first, but he got hard as the devil, so I piped down and let him think it was a man. Ever hear of such a thing?"

"Yes," said Mrs. Rogers, "I've heard considerable about it already this morning."

"How's that?"

"Oh, the children saw the parade, too."

"Oh, they did, huh? That's good. They didn't think that bear was a man, did they?"

"Willie thought it was a Russian," said Mrs. Rogers.

At quarter to eleven Miss Agnes Birdsong, high-school English teacher, was down on Main Street waiting for the parade and feeling a little foolish. She felt even more foolish when she saw what a silly little parade it turned out to be. But she looked pretty standing in the shade in her flimsy summer dress; she looked pretty, and she knew it, and she kept on standing there and watching.

She couldn't quite identify the animals at first. Then she said to herself: "Of course, that thing's a unicorn." Then she remembered that unicorns were figments of the imagination. "It's a fake," she corrected herself.

She regarded the snake with a slight feeling of illness. She hated snakes anyway; this huge grey yellow-tongued worm with scarlet throat and jeweled eyes bothered her and frightened her. Suppose it should get loose. Of course, it was penned in there, but suppose it should get loose. How terrible. The grinning old Chinaman, noting her concern, reached around behind him with his whip handle and prodded the serpent. It hissed like a truck tire going flat and shifted its slimy coils.

Miss Agnes shuddered.

Then she saw the sphinx and the old bearded man driving it and the man in the cage on the wagon. The old bearded man was wool-gathering; the reins lay listless in his hands; his thoughts, far away from Abalone and the business of driving in the parade, played gently in some stray corner of the universe of his mind. The sphinx, noting its driver's inattention, took the bit in its teeth, gave a sluggish leap, and almost snapped the reins from the old fellow's grasp.

"Pay attention to your business, Apollonius," snarled the sphinx.

Miss Agnes Birdsong nearly sat down on the sidewalk in amazement. She looked at the people around her, but they seemed not to have heard a word. Miss Agnes touched her pulse and her brow. "I am a calm, intelligent girl," she said firmly. "I am a calm, intelligent girl."

Then the last wagon came along drawn by the golden ass, driven by the clovenfooted satyr. A little gold ring was in the satyr's nose; beside him on the seat was his syrinx. To Miss Agnes he smelled like a goat. His torso was lean as a marathon runner's; his hoofs were stained grass-green. A grape leaf was caught in his hair. He leered at Miss Agnes; he shielded his eyes with his hand and leered at her. He turned in his seat and stared back at her, staring and staring as though out of his accumulation of years he could remember nothing to compare with her.

"I am a calm, intelligent girl," Miss Agnes reassured herself. "I am a calm, intelligent girl, and I have not seen Pan on Main Street. Nevertheless, I will go to the circus and make sure."

At a quarter past twelve, Mr. Etaoin, the *Tribune* proofreader, went around to the *Tribune* newsroom to see about getting a pass to the circus.

The city editor gave him one. "Old Chink brought 'em in this morning. Funny old bird. Spoke good English. Didn't want any free publicity for his show or anything. Said he understood it was customary for newspaper men to get in at all the shows and entertainments for nothing anyway, so he was bringing around a few passes to save trouble out at the grounds. Oh, by the way, Etaoin, did you see the parade this morning? I missed it, but from what I've heard it was a kinda screwy thing."

"It was unusual rather than screwy," said Etaoin. "Did you hear anything about a bear that looked like a man?"

"No," said the editor, "but I did hear something about a man that looked like a bear."

"That's just as good," said the proofreader.

"Well, what about this unicorn stuff?" asked the editor.

"Yeah, they had a unicorn, too."

"Oh, yeah? Seems to me I heard something about a sphinx, also."

"There was a sphinx there, too."

"Oh, yeah?"

"Uh huh. And the golden ass of Apuleius was there and the sea serpent and Apollonius of Tyana and the hound of the hedges and a satyr."

"Quite a collection," said the editor. "You haven't forgotten any of them, have you?"

Etaoin thought awhile. "Oh, sure," he said; "I did forget. There was that Russian."

At a quarter of two Mr. Etaoin started for the circus grounds intent on viewing the sideshows first before the big top opened up for the main performance. He had a pass good for everything anyway; there was no profit in not using it to the uttermost; no sense in not squeezing from it everything gratis that could be squeezed. Money was made to buy things with, but passes were designed to take you places for nothing. The freedom of the press.

It was hot as he walked through the streets of Abalone. Etaoin reflected how much better it was to have it so hot rather than correspondingly cold—it would be way below zero. Overcoats. Mufflers. Overshoes. Eartabs. And every time he'd go in a door the lenses of his glasses would cloud over with opaque frostiness, and he would have to take them off and regard things with watery eyes while he wiped them dry again. A pox on wintertime. A curse on cold weather. An imprecation on snow. The only ice Mr. Etaoin ever wanted to see again was ice in little dices made in electric refrigerators. The only snow he ever wanted to see again was the snow in newsreels. He wiped the perspiration from his brow and crossed to the shady side of the street. On the telephone wires birds perched, their bills hanging open in the terrific heat. Heat waves like cellophane contours writhed from building roofs.

By the time he reached the circus grounds he had almost forgotten the circus; and, as he walked up to the tents, he was at a loss to think what he was doing there in that dusty field under the red-hot sun at that time of day. Then over the pathway between the rows of tents he saw a big red and black banner. It proclaimed:

THE CIRCUS OF DOCTOR LAO

"So that's the name of it," thought Mr. Etaoin.

The tents were all black and glossy and shaped not like tents but like hard-boiled eggs standing on end. They started at the sidewalk and stretched back the finite length of the field, little pennants of heat boiling off the top of each. No popstands were in sight. No balloon peddlers. No noisemakers. No hay. No smell of elephants. No roustabouts washing themselves in battered buckets. No faded women frying hot dogs in fly-blown eating stands. No tent pegs springing up under one's feet every ninth step.

A few people stood desultorily about; a few more wafted in and around the rows of tents. But the tent doors all were closed; cocoon-like they secreted their mys-

terious pupæ; and the sun beat down on the circus grounds
of Abalone, Arizona.

Then a gong clanged and brazenly shattered the hot
silence. Its metallic screams rolled out in waves of irritating sound. Heat waves scorched the skin. Dust waves
seared the eyes. Sound waves blasted the ears. The gong
clanged and banged and rang; and one of the tents opened
and a platform was thrust out and a Chinaman hopped on
the platform and the gong's noise stopped and the man
started to harangue the people; and the circus of Doctor
Lao was on:

"This is the circus of Doctor Lao.
We show you things that you don't know.
We tell you of places you'll never go.
We've searched the world both high and low
To capture the beasts for this marvelous show
From mountains where maddened winds did blow
To islands where zephyrs breathed sweet and slow.
Oh, we've spared no pains and we've spared no dough;
And we've dug at the secrets of long ago;
And we've risen to Heaven and plunged Below,
For we wanted to make it one hell of a show.
And the things you'll see in your brains will glow
Long past the time when the winter snow
Has frozen the summer's furbelow.
For this is the circus of Doctor Lao.
And youth may come and age may go;
But no more circuses like this show!"

The little yellow wrinkled dancing man hopped about
on the platform sing-songing his slipshod dactyls and
iambics; and the crowd of black, red, and white men
stared up at him and marveled at his ecstasy.

The ballyhoo ceased. The old Chinaman disappeared.
From all the tents banners were flung advertising that
which they concealed and would reveal for a price. The
crowd lost its identity; the individual regained his, each
seeking what he thought would please him most. Mr.

Etaoin wondered just where to go first. Over him fluttered a pennant crying, FORTUNES TOLD. "I shall have my fortune told," Mr. Etaoin confided to himself; and he scuttled into the tent.

Miss Agnes Birdsong, high-school English teacher, arrived at the circus grounds ten minutes after two. She neatly parked her neat little coupé alongside the curb on the opposite side of the street, raised the windows, got out, locked the doors, and walked across the street to the multitude of tents.

On a platform in front of one of the tents the old bearded man who had been wool-gathering while he drove in the parade that morning was doing the ballyhooing. It was the poorest ballyhoo speech Miss Agnes had ever heard in all her life, and she had heard some terrible ones. The old man spoke in a thin, weak voice, apparently extemporaneously, for he often had to stop and think what to say next. He was talking about the sideshows:

". . . 'nd in that tent over there, the third one after the big one, you people will see the chimera, a very curious beast. I don't suppose any of you people know what a chimera is, but it doesn't matter; go and look at him anyway. He can't hurt you, of course; being penned up that way for so long has gentled his nature. I think he's shedding now, that is, the lion part of him is shedding, so he won't look so glossy, but you can still tell what he is, of course. And Doctor Lao will be around there somewhere to answer any questions you may want to ask regarding the chimera. A very curious beast. I understand they are very nearly extinct. I can't think where the doctor got this one. In the next tent is the werewolf, I believe; yes, the werewolf is in the next tent to the chimera. You all know what a werewolf is, I assume. Very interesting beast, indeed. Later on, in the month of October, it becomes a woman for six weeks. Period of metamorphosis is curious to watch. Too bad it isn't changing form now. Know you people would like to see a wolf change into a woman. We feed it lamb chops as a rule. However, Doctor Lao will tell you all about it over in the tent. He has a very interesting lecture on the werewolf, I understand. Really must listen to it myself sometime. I don't know a great deal about the beast, to be perfectly frank. Then, in another tent is the medusa. I myself perform magic tricks in the tent across the way. And, let me see, I'm sure you people would be interested in seeing the mermaid, because in this desert country away from the sea, these ocean-dwelling creatures are bound to be unusual. Then, too, there is the hound of the hedges, which probably you have never seen, because it is indigenous to grasslands and weed patches and hedgerows and the like. The show for men only is in the last tent. I imagine the fertility dance of the Negro priests will start presently. Of course, that tent is for men only.

"So glad to see so many of you people here this afternoon, and I am sure that Doctor Lao is likewise pleased. He went to a great deal of trouble to collect all these animals, and I know you will all be interested in the strange animals. Oh, yes, I forgot to tell you about the roc's egg. It's in another tent back there, I'm not sure just which one. It's a great big egg, big as a house almost, and sweats salt water. I'm sure you good people will be interested in seeing the roc's egg. Doctor Lao will give a lecture on it in the tent. I think it's the third tent there, but I'm not sure. I really must, I suppose, familiarize myself more with the position of the various exhibits. Well, I suppose you are all tired of hearing me talk and want to go look at the shows. Remember, I perform my magic in the tent just across the way."

The old man climbed painfully and slowly off the platform and pushed his way through the crowd to the tent where he did his magic. A few people followed in after him. Miss Agnes Birdsong stood undecided. Then out of the corner of her right eye she saw the old Chinaman scuttling along with a pot of tea in his hand and a pipe of opium in his mouth. She halted him.

"Doctor Lao?"

"Yes, lady."

"Where is the tent with Pan?"

"We do not have Pan in this circus, lady. What you are thinking of, no doubt, is the satyr who drove for us in the parade this morning. He is in that tent over there. Admission is ten cents. If you wish to see him, just pay me here and go right in. We are a little short-handed on ticket-takers at present."

Miss Agnes gave the Chinaman two nickels and, assuring herself she was a calm, intelligent girl, entered the tent to see the satyr.

He lay scratching himself on a rack of grapevines, his thin, wispy beard all messy with wine lees. His hoofs were incrusted with manure, and his hands were bony, gnarled and twisted, brown and rough and long-nailed. Between his horns was a bald spot surrounded by greying curly hair. His ears were sharp-pointed, and lean, thin muscles crawled over his arms. The goat hair hid the muscles of his legs. His ribs stuck out. His shoulders hunched about his ears.

He grinned at Miss Agnes, took up his syrinx, and started to play. Thin reedy piping music danced in the dull air in the dark tent. He arose and danced to his own music, his goat tail jerking shortly, prodding stiffly, wagging and snapping. His feet did a jig, the clicking hoofs keeping time to his piping, pounding the dirt floor, clacking, clicking, clucking. The goaty smell grew stronger.

Miss Agnes stood there assuring herself she was a calm, intelligent girl. The satyr capered around her, tossing his pipes, tossing his head, wriggling his hips, waggling his elbows. The syrinx peep, peep, peepled. The door of the tent fell shut. Around Miss Agnes the aged goat man galloped. His petulant piping screeched in her ears like the beating of tinny bells; it brought a nervousness that shook her and made her blood pump. Her veins jumping with racing blood, she trembled as Grecian nymphs had trembled when the same satyr, twenty centuries younger, had danced and played for them. She shook and watched him. And the syrinx peep, peep, peepled.

He danced closer, his whirling elbows touching with

their points her fair bare arms, his shaggy thighs brushing against her dress. Behind his horns little musk sacs swelled and opened, thick oily scented stuff oozing out—a prelude to the rut. He trod on her toe with one hoof; the pain welled up to her eyes, and tears came. He pinched her thigh as he scampered around her. The pinch hurt, but she found that pain and passion were akin. The smell of him was maddening. The tent reeked with his musk. She knew that she was sweating, that globules of sweat ran down from under her arms and dampened her bodice. She knew that her legs were shiny with sweat. The satyr danced on stiff legs about her, his bony chest swelling and collapsing with his blowing. He bounded on stiff legs; he threw the syrinx away in a far corner; and then he seized her. He bit her shoulders, and his nails dug into her thighs. The spittle on his lips mingled with the perspiration around her mouth, and she felt that she was yielding, dropping, swooning, that the world was spinning slower and slower, that gravity was weakening, that life was beginning.

Then the door of the tent opened and Doctor Lao came in.

"The satyr," he said, "is perhaps the most charming figure in the old Greek polytheistic mythology. Combining the forms of both man and goat, its make-up suggests fertility, inasmuch as both men and goats are animals outstanding in concupiscent activities. To the Greeks satyrs were, indeed, a sort of deification of lust, woodland dieties, sylvan demigods. And, as a matter of fact, groves and woodlots are today favorite trysting places for lovers intent on escaping censorious eyes.

"We caught this fellow near the town of Tu-jeng in North China close to the Great Wall. We caught him in a net by a little waterfall, a net which we had set for a chimera. Incidentally, although we did not know it at that time, it is impossible to catch a chimera in a net by reason of its fiery breath, which burns up the meshes. But more of that later.

"Satyrs are not omnivorous like man, but rather herbivorous like the goat. We feed this fellow nuts and berries and herbs. He will also eat lettuces and some cabbage. He has always refused onions and garlic seed, however. And he drinks nothing but wine.

"Notice that he has a gold ring in his nose. I cannot account for it. It was there when we first captured him, but I do not know how it got there.

"Note also that this satyr is a very old one. I doubt not that he is one of the original satyrs of ancient Hellas. Obviously, being half-gods, satyrs live a long, long time. I place this fellow's age at nearly two thousand three hundred years, although Apollonius, my colleague, is inclined to grant him even more. If he could talk, he might tell us some very curious things about his existence. How the encroachment of the hostile Christian deity drove him and his kind out of the Hellenic hills to seek refuge in unamiable lands. How some of his relatives went north into Europe to become strange gods, like Adonis becoming Balder, or Circe becoming one of the Lorelei, or the Lares Domestici becoming cuckoo clocks and mantel statuettes. Yes, he could tell much, I fancy.

"But most interesting of all would be the narration of his own journey into China, his bewilderment at the lacquer temples and prayer wheels, his disgust at the hot spiced Chinese wines, and his sadness at the footbound Chinese maidens who could not dance to his piping. Hey, the forlorn, lost demigod.

"Satyrs originated, I fancy, back in the old pastoral days when men stayed out in the hills with their flocks for long periods of time. Among other things, to amuse themselves and soothe their flocks, the shepherds would play on pipes such as this fellow has here with him. And, doubtless too, on the hills at night by their fires the shepherds would dream of love. Men do dream of love, you know; lonely men do. Well, they would dream of love, and their dreams would be of such potency that their very flocks would be colored by them. In the moonlight's magic, perhaps, a she-goat would be transformed into a charming girl. . . . And then in lambing time a strange, wee fellow would

be seen cavorting among the woolly babies. On his brow
he bears his mother's horns; his feet are hoofed like hers;
but for the rest he is a man. He grows up to become
scornful of the stodgy sheep and goats and shy of man.
He steals his father's lute and skips away. Simple folk see
him at dusk by a lakeside, and a new pastoral god is
born. . . .

"The satyr sits by some mirrored lake and plays, and
even the little fishes swarm about and mimic a dance, for
the music of the satyr's pipes is irresistible. He plays on
his pipes, and the leaves on the trees dance, and the worms
stick their heads out of their holes and writhe, and under
the rocks scorpion hugs scorpion in hot, orgiastic bliss. . . .
And, by and by, a nymph comes shyly to peep through
the vines. . . .

"But that was a long time ago, and this is an old, old
satyr. I doubt if he could do anything like that now. Let
us go on to the next tent and see the sea serpent. This way,
please."

The whole Rogers family came to the circus grounds a
little after two that afternoon. The children were excited
because they were about to see the circus; the mother was
buoyant because her husband had a job again.

"Now I aint got a heck of a lot of money," said papa,
"but we can see a sideshow or two, I reckon, and then go
on into the main show. What sideshow do you kids want
to see first?"

Unable to make up their minds, the children wrangled
peevishly among themselves.

"Tell you what," said Mrs. Rogers after listening to them
for a while; "let's go see that bear or man or Russian or
whatever it is. I really would like to see it just to find out
why it causes so many arguments."

Plumber John agreed; the family went in search of the
bear tent. They couldn't find it. Then Doctor Lao came
out on the platform again, recited his poem again, and
started to talk about the show again.

John Rogers went up beside the platform and called to

him: "Say, doc, where do you all keep the big bear at? We want to see it again. The one that was in the parade this morning."

"Me no savvee bear business," said the doctor and plunged on in his speech:

"In the tent to the right, ladies and gentlemen, you will find that world-famous thaumaturgist, Apollonius of Tyana, born contemporary with Christ. 'Socrates,' they used to say, 'leaves men on the earth, Apollonius transports them to heaven; Socrates is but a sage. Apollonius is a god.' Well, he's over there in the next tent ready to perform a miracle or two for your edification. You will find him an old, old man. He has been alive since the Christian era began, and his years are beginning to show on him. Also, he has but recently learned English; bear with him there and do not laugh at his mistakes. Remember, he is the man who remained silent for five whole years listening to the counsel of his heart, the man who conversed with the astrologers of Chaldea and told them things they had never dreamed, the man who prophesied the death of the Emperor Domitian, the man who underwent the eighty tests of Mithra. In the tent to the right, ladies and gentlemen. Ten cents admission. Children in arms free."

"Hey, doc," said Plumber Rogers again, "whereabouts is the big bear? We all wanta see it again."

"Me no savvee bear business," said Doctor Lao and continued:

"In this tent to my left, good people, is one of those startling women, a medusa. One look out of her eyes and you turn to stone."

The doctor opened the tent door behind him and revealed a stone figure.

"This is what is left of a person in the last town where we showed. He would not heed my warning to look only at the medusa's reflection in a mirror. Instead he sneaked behind the canvas guardrail and stared her straight in the face. And this, ladies and gentlemen, is what is left of him. He doesn't make a very good statue, does he? Let me implore you, ladies and gentlemen, when you go into that tent, for your own good, look at her only in the mirror. It is very distressing for us always to have one or two customers turned to stone at every performance, besides being very difficult to explain to the police. So, once again, I ask you to look only at the medusa's reflection, not at the lady herself."

John Rogers tweaked the hem of the doctor's gown. "We wanta see the big bear, doc, me and the wife and the kids. Which tent is it in?"

Doctor Lao frowned down on the plumber. "Whatsa mattah allee time talkee talk bear business? Me no savvee bear business. You no like this Gloddam show, you go somewhere else." The doctor spread wide his arms and swept on in his discourse:

"Possibly the strangest of all the animals in this menagerie, and certainly one which none of you should miss seeing, is that most unique of all beasts, the hound of the hedges. Evolved among the hedgerows and grassplots of North China this animal is the living, breathing symbol of greenness, of fecund, perennial plant life, of the transitional stage between vegetable and animal. The greatest scientists of the world have studied this hound and cannot decide whether he is fauna or flora. Your guess, ladies and gentlemen, is as good as the next. When you examine him, you will notice that, although his form is that of the usual dog, his various bodily parts are those of plants. His teeth, for instance, are stiff, thick thorns; his tail is a plait of ferns; his fur is grass; his claws are burrs; his blood is chlorophyll. Surely this is the weirdest beast under the casual canopy of heaven. We feed him hedge apples and green walnuts. Sometimes, too, though not often, he will eat persimmons. Let me advise you, good people, to see the hound of the hedges even though you must forgo seeing the mermaid or the werewolf. The hound is unique."

"I can't seem to get much information out of the old boy," said the plumber to his wife. "Let's look at something else first; then maybe we can find the bear later."

"Well," said Mrs. Rogers, "suppose we watch the magician. I think the children would like that."

So the plumber and his family went into the tent to the right to watch Apollonius perform. Except for the mage they were the only ones in the tent.

Apollonius looked at them dreamily as they filed in. "It will be ten cents apiece," he said. John Rogers handed him a half-dollar. The thaumaturge put the coin in an old cigar box and scratched his head thoughtfully. "Now what sort of magic would you be wanting to see?" he asked.

"I want to see you take a pig out of this bag," said Alice, holding up to him her little sack of candy.

"Elementary, my child, elementary," said Apollonius. He inserted two fingers into the mouth of the candy sack and drew out a Poland China shoat. It squealed and writhed and kicked its little legs. The magician handed it to Willie. "You keep this, lad. Feed it well. It ought to make good sidemeat some day."

"Oh, goodness," said Mrs. Rogers, "we haven't room for a pig, really. Our place is so small, you know."

"Um," said Apollonius. "What a pity." He took the pig away from Willie and shoved it back in the sack. "It was such a nice pig, too. What do you want me to do now?"

"Know any card tricks?" asked Mr. Rogers.

"A multitude of them," said Apollonius. He reached into a pocket of his gown, took out a pack of cards and shuffled them with one hand. The cards climbed and fell in graceful spirals and parabolas, pyramiding and mixing and disintegrating, but always returning into a neat square-sided pack.

"This is not magic," commented the wizard. "This is only manual dexterity. Shall I convert some wine into water for you?"

"Why not change water into wine?" asked the plumber.

"I can do that as readily," said the magician. He took up a beaker of water and mumbled over it. It changed color;

a soft vinous odor was diffused in the air. He handed the beaker to Mr. Rogers. "Try a sip."

John tasted it. "Sherry," he said.

Apollonius tasted it. "I'd call it muscatel," he corrected. "What do you say it is, madam?"

Mrs. Rogers tried the wine. "It's a little like that in church," she said thoughtfully. "Of course, that's the only wine I ever drank before, so I don't know how to compare it."

"Well, it's not sacramental wine," said Apollonius. "I'm sure of that. But drink it up before Doctor Lao sees it. He doesn't like to have alcohol on the grounds."

Edna Rogers tugged at her mother.

"Mother, have him do something we like," she pouted.

"Do you care for flowers?" asked Apollonius.

"A little," said Edna.

"Naw, we don't like 'em," said Willie.

"Oh, yes, make some flowers for the children," said Mrs. Rogers.

The thaumaturge made passes in the air, and pink rose petals fell all about the family and on their shabby shoulders. He made more passes, and violets grew about their feet. Black flowers, yellow edged, climbed the sides of the tent. Mauve flowers with fuzzy tops and thin green leaves sprang up among the violets. A great grey flower on a hairy stalk floated up over their heads. It had a beard like a goat. Spikes and spines clustered the edges of its uneven petals.

Apollonius regarded the big blossom in wonderment. "Goodness," he said, "I never made a flower like that one before in all my life. I wonder what kind it could be. Do you know, mister?"

"Naw," said the plumber. "I don't know a whole lot of flowers. Just the common kinds like dandelions and all."

"Well," said Apollonius, "it's a big brute, whatever it is."

"I think you do the cleverest tricks," said Mrs. Rogers. "Don't you, children?"

Touched to the quick, the mage said: "Oh, these aren't

tricks, madam. Tricks are things that fool people. In the last analysis tricks are lies. But these are real flowers, and that was real wine, and that was a real pig. I don't do tricks. I do magic. I create; I transpose; I color; I transubstantiate; I break up; I recombine; but I never trick. Would you like to see a turtle? I can create a very superior turtle."

"I do," said Willie. "I want to see a turtle."

The magician kicked away some of the violets until he came to the bare soil. Enough of this he scraped up to fill both hands. He molded the earth between his fingers, smoothing it and shaping it and patting it and rubbing it. It became yellow and thick and malleable.

"Oh, oh!" said Alice. "Look, it's changing into a turtle. Gee, that's a wonderful trick."

Apollonius placed the turtle on the ground. Its head was withdrawn into its shell. He tapped on its back with a twig. "That generally makes them stick their heads out," he explained.

After a moment or so of being tapped the turtle did stick its head out. But instead of a single head it produced two. The heads were side by side, joined to the neck like the forks of a stick. The two heads opened their four eyes and two mouths and yawned. Then each head tried to start in a different direction.

"Oh, goodness," said Apollonius, disgustedly, "I would botch the job just when I wanted to do a really neat piece of magic for you. Imagine making such a freak thing! Two heads! Really, I apologize. I'm ashamed at my ineptitude."

"Oh, that's all right," said the plumber. "I guess them things are kinda hard to make right anyway."

Some more people came crowding into the tent, Doctor Lao following them.

"Uh, Apollonius," whispered the doctor, "I promised these folks you would resurrect a man from the dead for them. You'll do it, won't you? They all expressed themselves as being very much interested in watching you at it."

"Why, certainly," the wizard whispered back. "But, doctor, have we got a corpse?"

"I'll go and see," said the old Chinaman.

The crowd of people milled around on the flowers and frightened the turtle so that it pulled its heads back into its shell again. A big fat woman stepped on it. She looked down to see what was under her foot.

"Good God Almighty, Luther, there's a turtle in here!" she screeched.

"Where? Where?" asked Luther nervously. "Where the hell is it, Kate?"

"Right under my feet," sobbed Kate.

"It won't hurt you," said Mr. Rogers. "It's a real tame turtle, I think."

Luther pulled Kate aside and stared down at the chelonian. "It don't look tame to me."

"It's got two heads; hasn't it, mother?" said Willie.

"By God, I knew there was something queer about it," said Luther.

Doctor Lao came back in the tent with a big bundle in his arms.

"I got one," he whispered to Apollonius.

"Now stand back, all you people, around the edges of the tent," directed the doctor. "Apollonius of Tyana is about to perform the greatest piece of magic in several centuries. Before your very eyes he will restore life to a lifeless corpse. Before your very eyes the dead will become quick again. And at no further cost to you than what you paid to enter this tent. Stand aside, ladies and gentlemen; stand aside, please! Give the man all the room he needs."

Apollonius stooped over and unrolled the bundle. A little shrivelled dead man, one who had been a laborer of some sort, was disclosed. He had on overalls, old worn army shoes with leather laces in them, a blue hickory shirt, and an old worn-out cowboy hat. In the leather sweat band of the hat were the initials "R.K." floridly delineated in indelible pencil. One of the leather shoe-strings in the man's old worn-out army shoes had been broken and retied in several places. The knots looked as if they might have been done by a seafaring man.

Apollonius placed the cadaver on its side, drawing the arms up above the head. He bent the knees and slightly spread the legs. The corpse looked as if it was sleeping in a very uncomfortable position.

Apollonius began to pray a low, thick prayer. His eyeballs turned dead green; thin, hazy stuff floated out of his ears. He prayed and prayed and prayed. To the subtle spirit of life he sent his terrible invocation.

Then all of a sudden, when everyone was most expecting it, the dead man came to life, sat up, coughed, and rubbed his eyes.

"Where the devil am I?" he wanted to know.

"You're at the circus," said the doctor.

"Well, lemme outa here," said the man. "I got business to attend to."

He got to his feet and started off with a slight limp.

Luther caught his arm as he made for the door. "Listen, mister," he asked, "was you really dead?"

"Deader than hell, brother," said the man and hurried on out of the tent.

At about two-thirty two policemen arrived at the circus grounds to look the show over and see that nothing inimical to the public interest took place. One of the cops was a big fat jolly ignorant-looking guy; the other was a tall thin ugly man. They wore uniforms, Sam Browne belts, sidearms and shiny, brass badges. Doctor Lao spotted them from afar and slipped up behind them.

"Whatsah mattah? Chase crook? Somebody steal? Whatsah mattah cops come this Gloddam place? This my show, by Glod!"

"Now don't get all excited," said the fat cop. "We just came out to look around a little. Jest keep yer shirt on, slant-eye. We ain't gonna arrest nobody unless they needs it. We're officers; how about us takin' in a few of these here sideshows?"

"Make yourselves at home, gentlemen," said Doctor Lao. "Go where you please when you please. I shall instruct the ticket-takers to let you in wherever you may choose to go."

"That's the way to talk," said the policeman. "Whattayah got that's hot right now?"

"The sideshows are all open. Go anywhere you please," said the doctor. "You must excuse me now; I must go and give my lecture on the medusa."

The cops wandered around a little, peering in tents and staring at people and nodding to their friends. They caught a little boy sneaking in under a tent, pulled him back, bawled him out, and sent him home in tears. Then they decided to see a sideshow or two.

"We'll jest go in one right after another so's not to miss anything," said the thin ugly cop.

"Right," said the fat ignorant-looking cop. "Ever see such a goofy circus?"

"Never," said his buddy. "Let's go in here."

They went in the medusa tent. The interior was tinted a creamy yellow, and pale silver stars spangled the yellowness. A big mirror hung on the far wall. Before the mirror was a canvas cubicle, the interior of which was reflected in the mirror. One could not see into the cubicle unless one looked in the mirror. Mirror and cubicle both were roped off so that no one could approach very near to either.

Sitting on a couch in the cubicle was the medusa paring her nails. Her youth was surprising. Her beauty was startling. The grace of her limbs was arousing. The scantiness of her clothing was embarrassing. A lizard ran up the canvas side of her enclosure. One of the snakes on her head struck like a whiplash and seized it. The other snakes fought with the captor for the lizard. That was bewildering.

"What in the devil kind of a woman is that?" demanded the big fat ignorant-looking cop.

"Ladies and gentlemen," said Doctor Lao, "this is the medusa. She is a Sonoran medusa from Northern Mexico. Like her Gorgon sisters, she has the power to turn you into stone if you look her in the eye. Hence, we have this mirror arrangement to safeguard our customers. Let me beg of you, good people, to be satisfied with a reflected vision of her and not go peeking around the edge of the canvas at her. If anybody does that, I forecast lamentable results.

"First of all, however, look at her snakes. You will notice that most of them are tantillas, those little brown fellows with black rings about their necks. Towards the rear of her head, though, you can see some grey snakes with black spots on them. Those are night snakes, Hypsiglena ochrorhyncus, as they are called in Latin. And her bangs are faded snakes, Arizona elegans, no less. One of the faded snakes just now caught a lizard which some of you may have seen. Her night snakes also eat small lizards, but the tantillas eat nothing but grubs and similar small worms; the feeding of them is sometimes difficult in colder climes.

"It was a doctor from Belvedere, I believe, who first pointed out that the snakes of a medusa were invariably the commoner snakes of the locality in which she was born; that they were never poisonous; that they embraced several different species; that they fed independent of the woman they adorned. This Belvederian doctor was interested primarily in the snakes and only secondarily in the medusa, so his observations, as far as sideshow purposes are concerned, leave much to be desired. However, I have made a study of this and several other medusas and, hence, am able to tell you a little about them.

"The origination of medusas is a puzzle to science. Their place in the evolutionary scale is a mystery. Their task in the great balance of life is a secret. For they belong to that weird netherworld of unbiological beings, salient members of which are the chimera, the unicorn, the sphinx, the werewolf, and the hound of the hedges and the sea serpent. An unbiological order, I call it, because it obeys none of the natural laws of hereditary and environmental change, pays no attention to the survival of the fittest, positively sneers at any attempt on the part of man to work out a rational life cycle, is possibly immortal, unquestionably immoral, evidences anabolism but not katabolism, ruts, spawns, and breeds but does not reproduce, lays no eggs, builds no nests, seeks but does not find, wanders but does not rest. Nor does it toil or spin. The members of this order are the animals the Lord of the Hebrews did not create to grace His Eden; they are not among the products of the six days' labor. These are the sports, the offthrows, of the universe instead of the species; these are the weird children of the lust of the spheres.

"Mysticism explains them where science cannot. Listen: When that great mysterious fecundity that peopled the worlds at the command of the gods had done with its birth-giving, when the celestial midwives all had left, when life had begun in the universe, the primal womb-thing found itself still unexhausted, its loins still potent. So that awful fertility tossed on its couch in a final fierce outbreak of life-giving and gave birth to these nightmare beings, these abortions of the world. Ancient man feebly represented this first procreation with his figurine of the Ephesian Diana, who had strange animals wandering about her robe and sheath and over her shoulders, suckling at her numerous bosoms, quarreling among the locks of her hair. Nature herself probably was dreaming of that first maternity when she evolved the Surinam toad of the isthmian countries to the south of here, that fantastic toad which bears its babes through the skin of its back. Yes! Perhaps through the skin of the back of the mighty mother of life these antibiological beings came forth. I do not know.

"Now this medusa here is a young one. I should place her age at less than one hundred years. Judges of women have told me she is unusually attractive, that she possesses beauty far more lovely than that possessed by the average human girl. And I concede that in the litheness of her arms, the swelling of her breasts, the contours of her face, there is doubtless much that would appeal to the artistic in man. But she is a moody medusa. Sometimes I try to talk to her, to find out what she thinks about sitting there regarding all the world reflected in a mirror, potentially capable of depopulating a city merely by walking down the streets looking at the passers-by.

"But she will not talk to me. She only glances at me in the mirror with boredom—or is it pity or amusement?—on her face and fondles her snakes, dreaming, doubtless, of the last man she has slain.

"I recall an incident of some years ago when we were showing in the Chinese city of Shanhaikwan, which is situated at the northern extremity of the Great Wall. The medusa and some of the other exhibits in my circus were slightly ill from a long sea voyage, and the whole circus had a droopy air about it that was simply devastating to the business. Well, we put up our tents in Shanhaikwan and thought to stay there awhile until our animals had recovered. It was summer, the mountain breeze from Manchuria was refreshing. There was no war in progress thereabouts for a wonder, for that is the most war-ridden spot in the whole world; and we decided to stay there awhile and try to regain our customary equanimity.

"Sailors were in the city, sailors from foreign countries who were off their warships on shore leave; and they came to see my circus. They were a gang of drunken swine, but they paid the money, and I let them in. They saw the medusa and, being asses, thought she was just a girl I had fitted out with a cap of snakes in order to fool people. As if one had to go to all that trouble to fool people! However, as I was saying, they thought the medusa was an imposture; but they were enamored of her beauty and, for a boyish lark, they planned among themselves to kidnap her one night, take her down on the beach, rape her, and then cast her aside.

"So one black night, when the moon was behind a cloudbank, these sailors came sneaking up to the circus grounds and with their knives sliced a hole in the medusa's tent and went in after her. The night being so dark that they could not see her face, they were safe enough for the time being, at least.

"Apollonius and I were returning from a wineshop and

realized what they were doing as we came staggering and
arguing to our tent. I was very angry and would have
loosed the sea serpent upon the ravishers; but Apollonius
said not to, that the moon would be out presently, and
then matters would take care of themselves. So I quieted
down, and we watched and waited.

"There were ten drunken sailors in the mob. Pale as
ghostflesh were their white uniforms in the black darkness.
As I say, they split the tent with their knives, seized the
medusa, gagged her, and carried her down to the beach.
Just when they got her past the dunes, the moon came
out from behind its veil. And I assume the sailors were
standing in a semicircle about the medusa, for next morning, when Apollonius and I went down there, ten stone
sailors were careening in the sand just as she had left them
after looking at them; and the drunken leers were still on
their silly, drunken faces. And still are for aught I know,
for those leers were graved in the living stone.

"I tell you, it does not pay to fool with a medusa. Are
there any questions anyone would like to ask? If not, I
suggest we go and look at the sphinx."

A big fat woman in the crowd said: "Well, I don't believe a word you say. I never heard so much nonsense
in all my living days. Turning people to stone! The idee!"

A little man beside her said: "Now, Kate, don't go
sounding off that way in front of all these people."

Kate said: "You shut up, Luther; I'll say what I darn
good and well please!"

Doctor Lao said: "Madam, the rôle of skeptic becomes
you not; there are things in the world not even the experience of a whole life spent in Abalone, Arizona, could
conceive of."

Kate said: "Well, I'll show you! I'll make a liar out of
you in front of all these people, I will!"

And Kate shouldered her way through the onlookers
to the roped-in canvas cubicle where lounged the medusa.

"In the name of the Buddha, stop her!" screamed Doctor
Lao.

But Kate bent under the guard rope and stuck her face

around the edge of the cubicle. "Hussy," she started to say. And before she could utter a third syllable, she was frozen into stone.

Later on, while everybody was stewing around wondering what to do about it, a geologist from the university examined Kate. "Solid chalcedony," he said. "Never saw a prettier variegation of color in all my life. Carnelian chalcedony. Makes mighty fine building stone."

Ed and Martha, the railroad traffic officer and his wife, brought their two sons to the circus at two twenty-five.

"Well," said Martha, "I never did see such a funny-looking circus in all my life. Are you sure we're at the right place, Ed?"

"Absolutely, my dear."

"Well, then, I suppose we better look at some of the sideshows. Here's a tent with a mermaid in it. Let's go in here."

"Well, I'll tell you, Martha, I hate to spend money on anything that's so obviously a fake. We both know there aint any such thing as a mermaid. Let's look around a little more. I don't mind being fooled if I don't know at the time that I am being fooled, but the very idea of spending money to see something I know good and well is a fake is somehow repugnant to me."

"Maybe it aint a fake, papa," offered Ed junior.

"Don't say 'aint,' dear," corrected mama patiently.

"Let's go look at the snake," suggested little Howard.

"Oooh, snakes make mother so nervous." Mama shuddered.

"Well, whatta we gonna do? Just stand around all the time?" asked Howard.

"Now don't go talking to your mother that way, or father'll switch some politeness into you when we get home," threatened the traffic officer.

Howard began to cry.

"And don't go turning on the weeps, either, or you'll get switched right now."

Howard ceased crying.

"Perhaps this hound of the hedges would be interesting," said Martha, looking at the legend on a banner streaming from a near-by tent.

"No," said Ed, "there's nothing to it. Only a dog painted green. I saw it in the parade this morning."

"Aw, gee, papa, let's look at something," begged Ed junior.

"Frankly, Martha," said Ed, "I don't believe there's anything here we want to see. We shouldn't have come. I never dreamed anyone would try to palm off on the public such a collection of foolishness."

Doctor Lao came by headed for the medusa exhibit.

"Whatsah mattah? You tink someblody makeum fool allah time. I no fool you. You come this place looky look; you looky look. By Glod, I no charge you nothing. You go in flor nothing; takeum whole dam family flor nothing. You see: I no fool you. This place no catchum fake. This my show, by Glod!"

He pushed the traffic officer and his family into the tent with the roc's egg and dashed on about his business.

"He's the boss of this circus," explained Ed embarrassedly to his wife. "I guess he got sore about what I said about everything being a fake. What in the world is this thing here?"

"The sign said it was the roc's egg," said Martha.

The egg loomed like a monolith before them. Pockmarks in its shell were as big as golf balls. They oozed a thin watery secretion.

"It looks like an egg all right," agreed Ed. "But it's preposterous that any egg could be so big."

"Well, it is that big, isn't it, papa?" asked Howard.

"I guess so, my boy; I guess so."

"Well, what do we do? Just stand here and look at it?" asked Ed junior.

"Now, don't be impatient, dear," said mama.

"I tell you what," said the traffic officer; "I've got it figured out, I believe. It's not an egg at all. It's made of concrete or something, and it is a fake. There couldn't be an egg that big."

"Well, it looks that big, papa," said Howard.

"Now, Howard," cautioned mama.

"Well, why does all the water run out of it?" asked Ed junior.

"Oh, lots of times concrete'll sweat in hot weather, if it's poorly made," said papa. "It's porous, see, and soaks up moisture on cool nights. Then when it gets hot like this afternoon, the moisture collects and runs out. Kinda like a water pitcher. Capillary action, they call it."

"Gee, papa, you know everything, don't you, papa?" said Howard.

"Well, I can tell a lump of concrete from an egg when I see it," admitted the traffic officer.

The egg began to emit creaking sounds. It seemed to move a little, and from its apex a noise of tapping came. "It's the heat expanding it," said papa.

The tapping became louder. An irritating scratching accompanied it. The egg shook and rolled a little. "Back up a little, everybody," said papa. "Looks like the thing was going to turn over."

A grating, tearing sound came from the top of the egg, and a hunk of shell fell off at their feet. A yellow bill the size of a plowshare stuck out of the egg.

"My God, it's hatching," said mama.

"Stand back, everybody," ordered papa.

The top of the egg splintered and crackled, and out of the ruptured opening a baby roc stuck its frowzy head and looked down at them. Silly pinfeathers, big as ostrich plumes, adorned its grey skin, and the yellow at the corners of its mouth was as yellow as butter. Then the egg fell all apart, and the roc chick stood weeping in the litter of eggshell. It opened its mouth and wailed with horrible hunger.

"Come on, let's get out of here," said the traffic officer.

"It wasn't really concrete, was it, papa?" asked Howard.

"Now, Howard, please don't ask any more questions," said mama.

Papa said: "Let's go on home, Martha. I don't like this place."

"All right," said Martha, smiling.

At the curb near the edge of the circus grounds a big truck prevented them from getting into their own car. Some rough-looking men were loading a big hunk of stone onto the body of the truck. The traffic officer recognized a man standing near the truck. He hailed him:

"Hello there, Luther! What did you do, buy a statue at the circus?"

Luther looked at him sourly. "That aint no statue," he said. "That's Kate."

"Epitomizing the fragrance of grassplots, lawns, and hedgy, thickset places, the behemoth of hounds stands unique in the mysterious lexicon of life. Most of the other curiosities of this circus, I regret to say, have a taint of evil or hysteria about them, but not this magnificent hound. He is as sweet as hay new mown with clover blossoms still unshriveled lying in it. He is as sunny as the dewy mornings his parent grasses so much love. He is a grand beast, if beast he may be called. Also, though I refer to him in the masculine gender, such designation is very loose; for, as a matter of fact, this hound has sex only as a water lily might have sex. He is alone of his kind throughout the world; no mate and no sire; no dam and no brood. This hound is no more masculine than a horse radish, no more feminine than a cabbage, less carnal than a tiger lily, and as little lustful as a rose bush.

"We found him in North China along the canals where the ricefields flourish and where grasses and little stunted hedges grow. For a long, long time that land had been nothing but so much parched dust with no green thing growing upon it anywhere. Then the canals were constructed and brought water to it, and over its dry skin lovely green things commenced to grow. That which had seemed dead quickened into life. That which had seemed sterile glistened with fertility. And as a symbol and embodiment of that exuberant fecundity, the grasses and the weeds and the flowers and hedges and bushes each gave a little of themselves and created this hound, truly an unparalleled achievement in the annals of horticulture.

"We saw him first at dusk playing about the hedgerows, leaping, gamboling, biting at the hedge apples, pawing little holes in the ground and nosing fugitive seeds into them. Alarmed by us he romped about in great tearing circles, flitting through the grasses and disappearing behind hedges so swiftly the eye could hardly follow him. His beautiful greenness entranced us. We had never seen so wonderful a hound in all the world.

"So we caught him. Out of his strange eyes he looked at us—eyes that were like green unripened pods. He was perfectly gentle. His tail of ferns wagged a little, switching his sides of green, green grass. From his panting mouth chlorophyll slavered. Around his neck a thin grass snake was curled, and his leafy ears harbored green katydids and tiny black crickets.

"In the meshes of our nooses he stood there regarding us. And, oh, that first close view of his great green glorious head! He was standing in the grasses, shoulder deep among the fresh green grasses; his parent grasses, the grasses that he loved. With their slim green fingers they caressed him and sought to shield him from us. They sought with their greenness to reabsorb his greenness, to hide him, to protect him; this their son. I tell you, nothing in the world has ever thrilled me as much as did the first sight of the hound of the hedges, and I have adored and studied animals for more than a hundred years. I said: 'Here is the masterwork of all life, here in this superb living body that is neither plant nor animal but a perfect balance of both. Here is a mass of living cells so complete in itself that it even demands no outlet for reproduction, content to know that, though it did reproduce its form a thousand times, it could never through that or through the evolutionary changes of a thousand generations improve upon its own victorious completeness.'

"Most immaculate of all was his conception among the humble weeds and grasses. All things trample them, devour them, plow them under and destroy them. But they endure and are beautiful and retain their gentleness and harbor no rancor. Yet once a great passion came to them, a pure passion not ever to be clearly understood; revolt was in it, and other things foreign to grasses; and out of that strange passion of the plants the hound of the hedges was conceived and born.

"And I wondered, too, for it had always been my belief that beauty was a modification of sex. Life sings a song of sex. Sex is the scream of life. Rutting and spawning the dance of life. Breed, breed, breed. Fill and refill the wombs of the world. Tumescence and ejaculation. Flinging out spore and seed and egg and bud. Quickening and birth. Sterility and death. That was life, I thought, and that was life's means to the end that finally, after almost infinite centuries of trial and error, there might be produced the perfect living thing.

"But here was this hound, product of no trial and error process, lacking lust, unhampered by ancestral fears and instincts. And I wondered if in this hound of the hedges were not to be found the apogee of all that life could ever promise. For here were beauty and gentleness and grace; only ferocity and sex and guile were lacking.

"And I wondered: 'Is this a hint of the goal of life?'"

Doctor Lao reached in the cage and patted the hound's head. The beast soughed like the murmur of wind in sycamore leaves.

"What the hell is the Chink talking about?" asked Quarantine Inspector Number One.

"I'll be damned if I know," said Quarantine Inspector Number Two. "Let's go see the mermaid. That goddam dog looks like a fake to me, somehow."

She lolled in her tank of salt water, her winnowing fishtail stirring salty bubbles that frothed and foamed about her slight breasts, and little bits of waterfoam clung to her fair wild hair. Her sea-green, sleekscaled fishtail arched in the water, and the fanlike fin on the end showed pink as a trout's. She sang a little lilting song of the far waves from which they had taken her, and the goldfish that swam with her in the tank poised on their nervous fins to listen. She laughed at the little red fishes, stirring them with her slender hands. They came to her and nibbled about her shoulders and swam in and out among the tresses of her water-lifted hair. Graceful as a fish she was and beautiful as a girl, and stranger than either; and the two quarantine inspectors were shocked because she wore no bathing suit.

"We found her in the Gulf of Pei-Chihli," said Doctor Lao. "We found her there on the brown, muddy waves. They were brown and muddy because inland it had rained and the little rivers had carried the silt out into the sea. And after finding her we came upon the sea serpent, and we captured him, too. It was a most fortunate day. But she pines sometimes, I think, for her great grey ocean. I hate to keep her penned up in this tank, but I know of nowhere else to put her. I think I shall turn her loose some day when we are showing along the seacoast. Yes, I shall take her out in the dawn when no one else is about and carry her down to the sea. Waist-deep in the water I'll go with her in my arms, and I'll put her down gently and let her swim away. And I shall stand there, an odd, foolish-looking old man, waist-deep in the water, mourning over the beauty I have just let slip away from me, mourning over the beauty I could touch and see but never completely comprehend; and, if anyone sees me there, waist-deep at dawn in the water, surely they will think me mad. But do you suppose that after she swims out a little ways she will turn and wave at me? Do you suppose she will blow a little kiss to me? Oh God, if I could only have seen her when I was a young man! The contemplation of her beauty might have changed my whole life. Beauty can do that, can't it?

"Yes, I think I will take her down to the sea and free her. And I will stand there and watch her swim out into the tide. But I wonder if she will turn and wave at me. Do you think she will, sir?"

"Uh, I couldn't say," said Quarantine Inspector Number Two.

"What do you feed her, doc?" asked Inspector Number One.

"Seafoods," said the doctor. "Let's go look at the sphinx."

The blunt-nosed woman-face of the thing stared at the two inspectors as they followed the Chinaman into the tent. The leonine tail switched softly at flies. "You bring the queerest people in here, Doctor Lao," said the sphinx reproachfully.

"It's all in the interest of the trade," said the doctor.

"Good Lord! Can it talk?" asked an inspector.

"Of course," said the doctor, while the sphinx looked bored.

"What is it, a he-sphinx or a she-sphinx?" asked the other inspector.

Doctor Lao was embarrassed. "Come outside and I'll tell you," he muttered.

Out of the tent he said to them secretively: "I wish you hadn't asked that in front of the sphinx. You see, it's neither man nor woman; it's both."

"Aw, how can it be?" asked the first inspector.

"Haven't you gentlemen ever heard of such a thing? Really, I'm amazed. A long time ago a man named Winkelmann found it out by looking closely at little African sphinxes. They are actually both male and female at the same time. The state of being bisexual, it is called."

"Well, I'll be durned," said Inspector Number Two. "Let's go back and look at that critter again, Al."

Frank Tull, the lawyer, telephoned his wife a little after two from his office and asked her if she wanted to go to the circus.

"No," she said, "but I advise you to go and take another good long look at that man you thought was a bear. Then maybe you'll realize how easy it is for people to see one thing and swear they saw something totally different when they get on the witness stand."

"Aw, honey," said Frank, "what the hell do you want

to be nasty for? I thought you had forgotten all about that by this time. I said it was a man, didn't I?"

"Yes, but you said it just to humor me. And if there's anything I hate, it's being humored, especially when I know I'm right."

"Well, I'll tell you what, dear: you come and go with me, and we'll both look at that thing again, and whichever of us was wrong will apologize to the other. How's that?"

"My God, Frank, I know perfectly well it was a man! I see no necessity for going out to that hot circus just to convince myself all over again. But you go, and I will be very gracious about it when you come home and apologize to me for sneering at me the way you did this morning."

"You are being very unreasonable, darling."

"On the contrary, I conceive myself as being the acme of reasonableness, considering the way you cackled at me, and all those horrid things you said about my needing glasses. If I had acted according to the promptings of my indignation I would have caused a scene that might have ended only in the divorce courts."

"Listen, honey, are you really still sore about that parade, or are you just kidding me?"

"No, I'm not sore, Frank. But neither am I kidding."

"Well, I wish you'd change your mind and go."

"No, Frank, really I don't care about seeing it. You go on by yourself and have a good time, dear."

"Well . . . good-by."

"Good-by."

So Frank told his stenographer to tell any of his clients who might call on him that he would be back in half an hour, and he went out and got in his sedan and drove down Main Street to the circus grounds.

A man of many artificial parts was Lawyer Frank Tull. His teeth had been fashioned for him and fitted to his jaws by a doctor of dental surgery. His eyes, weak and wretched, saw the world through bifocal lenses, so distorted that only through them could the distortion of Frank's own eyes perceive things aright. He had a silver plate in his skull to guard a hole from which a brain tumor had been removed. One of his legs was made of metal and fiber; it took the place of the flesh-and-blood leg his mother had given him in her womb. Around his belly was an apparatus that fitted mouth-like over his double hernia and prevented his guts from falling out. A suspensory kept his scrotum from dangling unduly. In his left arm a platinum wire took the place of the humerus. Once every alternating week he went to the clinic and was injected either with salvarsan or mercury according to the antepenultimate week's dose to prevent the Spiro-chæta pallida from holding too much power over his soul. Odd times he suffered prostate massages and subjected himself to deep irrigations to rectify another chronic fault in his machinery. Now and then, to keep his good one going, they flattened his rotten lung with gas. On one ear was strapped an arrangement designed to make ordinary sounds more audible. In the shoe of his good foot an arch supporter kept that foot from splaying out. A wig covered the silver plate in his skull. His tonsils had been taken from him, and so had his appendix and his adenoids. Stones had been carved from his gall, and a cancer burnt from his nose. His piles had been removed, and water had been drained from his knee. Sometimes they fed him with enemas; and they punched a hole in his throat so that he could breathe when his noseholes clogged. He carried his head in a steel brace, for his neck was broken; currently also his toenails ingrew. As a member of the finest species life had yet produced he could not wrest a living from the plants of the field, nor could he compete with the beasts thereof. As a member of the society into which he had been born he was respected and taken care of and lived on, surviving, no doubt, because he was fit. He was a husband but not a father, a married man but not a lover. One hundred years after he died they opened up his coffin. All they found were strings and wires.

He parked his car, got out of it, and walked across the street to the circus to look at its freaks.

The chimera lay sleeping on a pile of freshly turned

clay, and it coughed in its sleep; and the fetor of its belching, wafting upwards, asphyxiated the gnats that swarmed about its head. Little dead denizens of the lower air strata, they fell like floating flakes of powder, and no requiem accompanied their falling. The sleeping chimera kicked in his sleep, following the dictates of some action-filled dream; and the great claws of his paws lacerated the clay upon which he slept. His eagle wings half spread, their pinions expanding fanwise, and, all rumpled, they drew together again, the feathers tangled and fluffy. His dragon tail stirred snakelike, and the metal barb of its tip plowed up little furrows in the clay. His whiskers were singed where his fire-breath had scorched them. Some of the scales on his tail were gangrened and sloughing off where a colony of parasites bred and pullulated. He was shedding; great loose patches of fur, like hunks of felt, hung from his hide. Ticks crawled about in and over those patches. He had a nasty minkish smell, keenly sweetish, fattily pukish, vile and penetrating.

Frank Tull, the lawyer, stood there and stared at the chimera and was horrified to perceive that it was not a fake after all.

"By Gawd!" said one of the quarantine inspectors, "I never thought there was no sech animal."

The sleeping chimera gave a great snort; sparks, soot, smoke, and flame frothed out of his nostrils.

"That's why we have to bed him down on clay," said Doctor Lao. "If we let him sleep on hay, he'd burn it all up. Do you know how he manages that fire-breathing trick? Well, sir, it's simple when you understand his metabolism. You see, the chimera, like Arizona's outstanding citizen, the Gila monster, has no elimination system in the sense that ordinary animals have. Instead of expelling waste matter through the bowels, he burns it up within him, and he snorts out the smoke and ashes. Yes, a chimera is its own incinerator plant. Very unusual beast."

"What makes you think Gila monsters have no elimination system?" asked Mr. Etaoin.

"Well, that's what everybody around here claims," said

the doctor. "A hell of a lot of people have told me that. Seems that's how the Gila monsters get their poison: the waste matter in them having no outlet, it concentrates and intensifies and putrefies and works into their saliva so that when one of the big lizards bites anyone he thereby poisons him. Quite an interesting theory, I think. I much prefer its piquancy to a more rational explanation of Heloderma's venomous attributes."

"Well, however did you ketch this here shimmerra, doctor?" a country lass wanted to know.

"Oh, we got him years ago in Asia Minor. Chimeras have one frailty: they are enamored of the moon. So we took a mirror, placed it on a mountain top where it reflected the midnight moonlight, and the lunar-loving monster thought his bright silver ball was in reach at last. Well, sir, he came soaring and screaming down out of the heavens, crashed into the mirror, and us boys we jumps out, and over his shoulders we flings a golden chain. We had him!"

"Oh, Doctor Lao!" said a woman reporter from the *Abalone Tribune*, "I do so hope you will give me an interview sometime and tell me all about your wonderful adventures!"

"They'd make front-page news all right in a hick town like this," affirmed Doctor Lao.

An old-like, wealthy-looking party in golf pants and sport shirt and plaid socks probed at the chimera with his walking cane. The monster peevishly switched his tail like a horse switching at flies, raking the cane out of the old-like party's hand and sloughing him across the shins with the metal-barbed tip.

"Don't be foolin' with that animal, mister," warned Doctor Lao.

"What do you feed him?" somebody asked.

"Rattlesnakes," said the doctor.

"Lots of rattlers around Abalone here," said one of the quarantine inspectors. "I killed a hellbellin' big sidewinder down towards Beeswax last spring."

"You must be mistaken, friend," said Doctor Lao. "Sidewinders do not attain to any great size. In fact, they are among the smallest of the crotaline snakes."

"Well, this one was bigger than hell, by God," asserted the quarantine inspector.

"What I can't understand," said the old-like party in the golf pants, "is how in the world one animal can combine in itself the attributes of a lizard, an eagle, and a lion, as does this chimera, and have them all so perfectly blended together. Now, I cannot tell where the lion leaves off in this beast and where the lizard begins, nor where the eagle starts in; yet there they all three are in a balanced combination. What sort of lizard would you say is incorporated in the monster's make-up, Doctor Lao? Could it be one of those Central American monitors, or iguanas as they are called?"

"Me no savvee lizard talk," said the old Chinaman.

"Maybe it's the beast of the Apocalypse," remarked Lawyer Frank Tull, who felt that he should remark something and not stand there forever silent like an idiot or a damn fool.

"Nothing of the sort," replied the old-like party in the golf pants. "We all know there never was such a thing. Biblical baloney, if you will permit me to say so, my dear sir. Biblical baloney. Sheer and unadulterated biblical baloney. Yes, sir, biblical baloney. You'll find lots of it in the old book."

"Well, my daddy claims the Bible's a mighty fine book," said the country lass.

"The chimera," said Doctor Lao, "flies high on tireless pinions; so high, indeed, that mortal man is rarely vouchsafed a glimpse of him. Years ago, in the Asia Minor campaigns of the great Iskander, one of the Macedonian captains killed a chimera with his longbow. He took it back with him to the museum at Alexandria, and there to preserve it for posterity, it was mounted by some forgotten Egyptian taxidermist. Years later, a monk from Tibet saw it in the museum and, on returning to his lamasery, made a statue of it in porcelain and set it out to decorate the yard. Still later, a Chinese, coming to that part of the country from the Northern Capital, saw the strange figure and took measurements of its proportions. Returning to his home, he fashioned another statue in bronze and presented it to Kublai, then great khan of all the Mongols. Then, when Kublai had the Tatar wall constructed in a square about the Northern Capital, he also ordered an astronomical tower built upon its eminence. In the tower were placed various instruments, yardstick arrangements for measuring the stars. And for the decorative motif to be worked into the design of these instruments, Kublai ordained that the figure of the chimera be used. This was done. Nowadays, one may still see chimeras in bronze writhing around celestial globes and holding in their claws celestial computing rods.

"Other Chinese kings, coming there from time to time, saw these chimeras, wondered at them, understood their significance not, and went away thinking that somehow the beasts symbolized the power of the great khan. Then the petty Chinese princes commenced using the chimera motif themselves and had it worked into the designs of their own royal decorations. About that time the misleading name of dragon was coined to designate this royal emblem, and wrongly, of course, the dragon was taken to mean ferocity. But the chimera of Kublai was a benevolent beast, a patron of the arts of contemplation and study; and it must have been surprised when later it found itself spraddled on a banner, going to war.

"Afterwards, when other lesser kings supplanted Kublai, one of them decided that his particular dragon should have five toes and that the dragons of other kings might have three toes, four toes, or even six or seven toes, but not five. A rival king disobeyed this edict, and war ensued. I forget how the war came out. You will notice that this chimera of mine, however, has four toes on his front feet and three on his rear, so the dogmatic king, if he supposed he had authenticity to back his claims, was very much mistaken. I never thought to count the toes on Kublai's chimeras in Peking, so I can't say whether the ancient sculptors were accurate."

"Will chimeras breed in captivity?" asked the lawyer.

"Oh, certainly," said the doctor. "They'll breed any time. This fellow here is always trying to get at the sphinx."

"Well, that isn't exactly what I mean, though, of course, it's interesting to know. I meant will they reproduce?"

"How can they, when they are all males?"

"What? Are there no female chimeras?"

"Not a single one, and very few males either, for that matter. You are looking at a rare animal, mister."

"Well, if there are no females, then where do they come from?"

"This one came from Asia Minor, as I already said a moment ago."

"Oh, hell! I mean how are they born?"

"Your question is unanswerable. No one knows the least detail of the life cycle of the chimera."

"Could it not be that the female chimera, like the females of several insect species, is of an entirely different bodily make-up from the male and, so far, has not been identified as such by science?" asked the old-like party in the golf pants.

"Science does not even recognize the existence of the male chimera, let alone search for its mate," said Doctor Lao.

"What is science, anyway?" asked the country lass.

"Science?" said the doctor. "Why, science is nothing but classification. Science is just tagging a name to everything."

The chimera awoke. The mists of sleep glazed his green eyes, and reflections of strange dreams swam and receded in his brain. Raising a hind foot he scratched at his tick-crawling hide and, done with the scratching, sniffed at the claw that had scourged the ticks. Doctor Lao took a rattle-snake from a large canister and tossed it to the chimera. The rattler fell in a heap, arched its head, whirred and buzzed and shifted its coils and defied the monster.

The chimera regarded the rattler as intently as a scullion maid regards a cockroach she is about to step on. Then he flung his tail high up over his back, as does a scorpion, and leaning forward, still as does a scorpion, struck the viper a smart blow on its head with the metal tip of his tail, also as would a scorpion. The rattler died. The chimera picked it up in his forepaws and, sitting kangaroo-like on his haunches, devoured the snake, nipping off the rattles with his front teeth and nicely spitting them aside. He ate the rattler a bite at a time as a child eats a banana and with every whit as much satisfaction. Done with the meal, the monster groveled before Doctor Lao, snorting smoke rings and begging for more food.

"No, my pretty thing; one snake a day is all you get in this hot weather," said the aged Chinese.

"You know," he continued to his audience, "it is very necessary to watch our animals' diet down here in Arizona. I think it is because of the lack of humidity or something. Although it may very well be nothing but the dust. Anyhow, if we overfeed them, they invariably have colic or, what is worse, worms. This chimera, of course, with his peculiar interior incinerating system burns the worms up as fast as they attack him. But take our sphinx, for instance. It is a homeric task to worm a sphinx. Ordinary vermifuges won't do at all. It takes a profoundly powerful purgative in large, incessant doses. The last time I wormed the sphinx it voided some of the strangest-looking worms I ever saw in my life. Just like enormous noodles they were. And now every time I look at noodles I think of those wretched tapeworms, and every time I look at tapeworms I think of noodles. It's very distressing."

"The noodle is a favorite Chinese dish, too, is it not?" asked the old-like party in the golf pants.

"I prefer shark fins," said Doctor Lao.

The widow Mrs. Howard T. Cassan came to the circus in her flimsy brown dress and her low shoes and went direct to the fortuneteller's tent. She paid her mite and sat down to hear of her future. Apollonius warned her she was going to be disappointed.

"Not if you tell me the truth," said Mrs. Cassan. "I particularly want to know how soon oil is going to be found on that twenty acres of mine in New Mexico."

"Never," said the seer.

"Well, then, when shall I be married again?"

"Never," said the seer.

"Very well. What sort of man will next come into my life?"

"There will be no more men in your life," said the seer.

"Well, what in the world is the use of my living then, if I'm not going to be rich, not going to be married again, not going to know any more men?"

"I don't know," confessed the prophet. "I only read futures. I don't evaluate them."

"Well, I paid you. Read my future."

"Tomorrow will be like today, and day after tomorrow will be like the day before yesterday," said Apollonius. "I see your remaining days each as quiet, tedious collections of hours. You will not travel anywhere. You will think no new thoughts. You will experience no new passions. Older you will become but not wiser. Stiffer but not more dignified. Childless you are, and childless you shall remain. Of that suppleness you once commanded in your youth, of that strange simplicity which once attracted a few men to you, neither endures, nor shall you recapture any of them any more. People will talk to you and visit with you out of sentiment or pity, not because you have anything to offer them. Have you ever seen an old cornstalk turning brown, dying, but refusing to fall over, upon which stray birds alight now and then, hardly remarking what it is they perch on? That is you. I cannot fathom your place in life's economy. A living thing should either create or destroy according to its capacity and caprice, but you, you do neither. You only live on dreaming of the nice things you would like to have happen to you but which never happen; and you wonder vaguely why the young lives about you which you occasionally chide for a fancied impropriety never listen to you and seem to flee at your approach. When you die you will be buried and forgotten, and that is all. The mortician will enclose you in a worm-proof casket, thus sealing even unto eternity the clay of your uselessness. And for all the good or evil, creation or destruction, that your living might have accomplished, you might just as well never have lived at all. I cannot see the purpose in such a life. I can see in it only vulgar, shocking waste."

"I thought you said you didn't evaluate lives," snapped Mrs. Cassan.

"I'm not evaluating; I'm only wondering. Now you dream of an oil well to be found on twenty acres of land you own in New Mexico. There is no oil there. You dream of some tall, dark, handsome man to come wooing you. There is no man coming, dark, tall, or otherwise. And yet you will dream on in spite of all I tell you; dream on through your little round of hours, sewing and rocking and gossiping and dreaming; and the world spins and spins and spins. Children are born, grow up, accomplish, sicken, and die; you sit and rock and sew and gossip and live on. And you have a voice in the government, and enough people voting the same way you vote could change the face of the world. There is something terrible in that thought. But your individual opinion on any subject in the world is absolutely worthless. No, I cannot fathom the reason for your existence."

"I didn't pay you to fathom me. Just tell me my future and let it go at that."

"I have been telling you your future! Why don't you listen? Do you want to know how many more times you will eat lettuce or boiled eggs? Shall I enumerate the instances you will yell good-morning to your neighbor across the fence? Must I tell you how many more times you will buy stockings, attend church, go to moving picture shows? Shall I make a list showing how many more gallons of water in the future you will boil making tea, how many more combinations of cards will fall to you at auction bridge, how often the telephone will ring in your remaining years? Do you want to know how many more times you will scold the paper-carrier for not leaving your copy in the spot that irks you least ? Must I tell you how many more times you will become annoyed at the weather because it rains or fails to rain according to your wishes? Shall I compute the pounds of pennies you will save shopping at bargain centers? Do you want to know all that? For that is your future, doing the same small futile things you have done for the last fifty-eight years. You face a repetition of your past, a recapitulation of the digits in the adding machine of your days. Save only one bright numeral, perhaps: there was love of a sort in your past; there is none in your future."

"Well, I must say, you are the strangest fortuneteller I ever visited."

"It is my misfortune only to be able to tell the truth."

"Were you ever in love?"

"Of course. But why do you ask?"

"There is a strange fascination about your brutal frankness. I could imagine a girl, or an experienced woman, rather, throwing herself at your feet."

"There was a girl, but she never threw herself at my feet. I threw myself at hers."

"What did she do?"

"She laughed."

"Did she hurt you?"

"Yes. But nothing has hurt me very much since."

"I knew it! I knew a man of your terrible intenseness had been hurt by some woman sometime. Women can do that to a man, can't they?"

"I suppose so."

"You poor, poor man! You are not so very much older than I am, are you? I, too, have been hurt. Why couldn't we be friends, or more than friends, perhaps, and together patch up the torn shreds of our lives? I think I could understand you and comfort you and care for you."

"Madam, I am nearly two thousand years old, and all that time I have been a bachelor. It is too late to start over again."

"Oh, you are being so delightfully foolish! I love whimsical talk! We would get on splendidly, you and I; I am sure of it!"

"I'm not. I told you there were no more men in your life. Don't try to make me eat my own words, please. The consultation is ended. Good afternoon."

She started to say more, but there was no longer anyone to talk to. Apollonius had vanished with that suddenness commanded by only the most practiced magicians. Mrs. Cassan went out into the blaze of sunshine. There she encountered Luther and Kate. It was then precisely ten minutes before Kate's petrification.

"My dear," said Mrs. Cassan to Kate, "that fortuneteller is the most magnetic man I ever met in my whole life. I am going to see him again this evening."

"What did he say about the oil?" asked Luther.

"Oh, he was frightfully encouraging," said Mrs. Cassan.

Influenced by liquor as they had never been influenced by the Young Men's Christian Association, the two college youths from back East, Slick Bromiezchski and Paul Conrad Gordon, came into the circus uttering wisecracks and having a hell of a good time generally.

Doctor Lao saw them at long range and came dashing up. "Whatsah mattah Glod damn college punks come this place?" he demanded. "You no savvee nothing here. Glet to hell out! This my show, by Glod!"

They laughed at the little old man's frenzy, threatening to sic the Japs on him if he didn't pipe down. They quoted laws they made up on the spot to show him he couldn't prevent anyone who paid from looking at his circus. Advising him to give up trying to be a Barnum and to go back to washing the smells out of shirt-tails, they wended their way to the peepshow and forgot him.

The peepshow was within a small tent off by itself. A curtain in the tent had holes punched in it at various heights to accommodate the eyes of men of varying stature. Through one of the holes an old-like party in golf pants was staring; through another a quarantine inspector was trying to get his eyes focused; the remaining holes were vacant of peepers.

The college youths each selected a hole that suited his ocular altitude, hunched over, and stared and stared.

Around an old grass hut three Negro priests were dancing beneath a symbol of striking masculinity. It was a rain dance, and a drizzle accompanied their posturings. They threw off their grass skirts, dancing nude under the huge lingam, their black hides greasy with the rain.

Out of the hut five maidens came, black maidens, lean and virginal and luscious. The priests pounced upon them and stripped them, and flung away dancing; the double thud of drums came mumbling through the rain. The black girls danced among the priests, stumbling and limping as the chaff and stubble on the ground bit into their feet. Black bodies bounded in the grey wetness.

The double thud of drums drummed louder, and the priests danced more madly; but exceeding even their ardor, the wenches snatched long willow withes from trees and flailed the black priestly hides, the withes cutting pink stripes along the ordained backs and bellies; and the double thud of drums came roaring down through the pouring rain, and the black priests howled and postured from the hot, queer pain of the maidens' lashings.

The great lingam shook and trembled; the grey dust of the rain settled like ashes on the black skins; the wind laughed and screamed; the rain ceased; and out of the forest stalked Mumbo Jumbo thumping a tomtom.

Under an amorphously soft glowing rainbow came Mumbo Jumbo; and the black Corybants kotowed and groveled and salaamed and genuflected and hunkered down and made obeisance. He spat on their godpraising shoulders.

The wenches eyed him and wiggled at him, made coy signs to him and trembled lasciviously. Mumbo Jumbo examined them carefully, felt and prodded and punched and pinched them. And he squeezed and rubbed and tickled and bit them. And he kissed them and rubbed their noses and pulled their ears and tasted their tongues and smelled their breaths and fingered them; and the wenches endured it all and snuggled up to him and warmed against him. But they pleased him not. He took up a club and beat them down into the mud; and he jabbed and poked the priests to their feet, and into their cowed faces he yelled his disapproval.

They huddled together and mumbled amongst themselves. One came cringing up to the god, making placating passes at him. Mumbo Jumbo struck him beside the rejected virgins.

Then the other priests slunk into the grass temple and emerged carrying a cross upon which was bound a fair-haired Nordic girl. They dropped her at the god's feet and fled. Mumbo Jumbo looked down upon her and was pleased. He unloosed her from the cross, picked her up by the hair, and under the still amorphously soft glowing rainbow, disappeared into the forest.

"Whoopee!" yelled Paul Conrad. "Boy, do I envy that big coon!"

"Oh, shut up!" said the old-like party in the golf pants. "Can't you damned punks look at anything without talking your fool heads off? Where the hell do you think you are, anyway; back on the campus?"

"Well, if you don't like our style, grampaw, why, you know what you can do about it," said Slick Bromiezchski.

"For once you said something intelligent," replied the old-like party. "I'm going to complain to the management." And he went barging out of the tent.

"Imagine complaining to the management of this outfit," chortled Paul.

"Just imagine," chortled Slick.

Laughing tranquilly, the college men returned to their peepholes.

Nymphs lay about on grey rocks, fat young nymphs with stomachs like washerwomen's and hips like horses'. Out in the rushes by the sea's edge the faun stood watching them.

Pink and white and young, and shy with the innocence of youth was the faun, pretty as a little choirboy without his cassock and hymnal. He stood amid the green rushes and watched the fat, lewd girls, who knew he was watching them. And they laughed and flounced about and did obscene things to one another, and the little faun parted the green rushes the better to watch them.

Two nymphs danced, the others laughing at them and urging them on; and all the nymphs watched the faun out of the corners of their eyes as he trembled among the rushes. But he only watched; he would approach no closer; and they called jeeringly to him and dared him to come play with them. But he shook his head, remaining where he was.

The nymphs lolled about, pawing at each other; and each nymph hoped that the others would leave so that she alone might go down to the faun. Then he came out of the rushes and up on the sand a little way, and from behind a rock, ready to leap away, watched them. They pretended to disregard him, knotting flowers in their hair, tossing sand on one another's shoulders, squatting about awkwardly and laughing shrilly. One threw a bee on her sister, and the bee stung, and the sister wept and then rose furiously to her feet; and the two nymphs fought as girls fight, weeping and scratching and biting and clawing. And the others threw sand at them and laughed and urged them on. And the little faun crept up a little closer.

One of the girls took a bunch of grapes in her hand and, offering them to him, walked toward him slowly. Her soiled feet shuffled in the dry sand, her frowzy hair hung in knots and snarls, and there were smudges and bruises on her thick legs. She held out the shriveled, rotten grapes to him, and grinned with her fat mouth at him, but revulsion came over him and he retreated toward the sea. There was sadness in her eyes as she threw away the fruit and returned to her sisters.

Her sisters mocked her and mimicked her. Angry, she seized a stick and hit at them; they rolled away from her, laughing. But out of the corners of their eyes they watched the faun.

Then the prettiest of them, the slenderest, the cleanest,

the most desirable, the freshest, left the others and walked off toward a far point of the sea. And her sisters, pretending not to notice her, started dancing again and singing, and now and then calling to the faun. On his haunches he sat and watched them uneasily; but he would not call back to them, and he would not join them.

They waved green branches at him, and tossed little shells to him, and called him names, and made faces at him. They joined hands, dancing in a circle round a flower bush.

The nymph that had left them skirted along the far beach. Then, hidden by the rushes, she entered the water and, knee-deep in the shallow sea, screened by the lush reeds, she waded up behind the faun. And the circle of nymphs, dancing with joined hands, danced slowly closer to him. He crouched there watching them, and he trembled.

She came out of the water softly without splashing and stole up behind him. The other girls broke the dance and sprang down at the faun. He leaped to make for the sea, but the pretty nymph was upon him. She caught him by the hands.

And the fat, lewd girls enclosed him in a circle of their riotous flesh, touching their uncleanliness against his white skin, pawing him with their lascivious fingers, and snatching him from one another that they might kiss his mouth with a kiss of lust and shame.

He fought against them bitterly and boyishly, striking at them angrily, yet weakly, as though he were afraid of hurting them; and there was something in his face that was not bitterness or anger; and sometimes when his hands fell on them they felt a caress instead of a blow.

He dropped down on the sand. They knelt squealing and simpering about him. In the tangle of arms and legs one of the faun's hands crept up and palped the pretty nymph's round bosoms.

"Boyoboy," snickered Slick, "I wonder what word the Greeks had for that!"

Outside the tent the voice of the old-like party in the

golf pants said complainingly, "They're in there, Doctor Lao, both of them. Half drunk and abusive. If you value the feelings of the rest of the people who want to look at your show, you'll chase them away from the grounds."

"Me fix 'em!" said the doctor. "Glod damn punks! Me fix 'em. Hey, Lube! Hey, Lube!"

"We're about to get the bum's rush," giggled Paul Conrad.

Into the tent something big and black and hairy came storming and grabbed the two college youths and yanked them out. Through the circus grounds it dragged them to the curb of Main Street, and out in the street on their ears it tossed them. And whether it was a man or a bear or a Russian no man could say, but plenty of men argued profanely about it.

"Damned best job of bouncing I ever saw in my life," commented the quarantine inspector to the old-like party in the golf pants. "Let's go back and look at that peepshow again, old-timer. Some of that stuff is kinda interesting."

Mr. Etaoin contemplated the sea serpent, and the sea serpent contemplated Mr. Etaoin. Mr. Etaoin lit a cigarette and blew grey smoke. The sea serpent exserted its tongue and flickered it; a long yellow naked nerve of a tongue, big as a man's hand, wrist, and arm, languidly sentient, gracefully forked, taster of sounds, feeler of vibrations, symbol of strange senses, silent and secret, suggestive of evil that harked back to Eden. Mr. Etaoin's eyes, circumscribed by rings of horn, looked at the snake through dustspeckled glass ovals. The serpent's eyes, lidless and fixed, regarded the proofreader with catlike pupils, thin black ellipses standing on end in fields of copper. The proofreader's eyes were dull, muscle-bound green things. The snake's eyes were sombre, rare, and wicked jewels.

Bored with the mutual examination, the snake slowly looped about its enormous cage, the convolutions of its body and tail following through the invisible pathway previously described by its head. Head rearing, it tested the interstices and reticulations of the steel latticework that kept it captive, hoping listlessly to find an opening it had overlooked before, searching the confines of its jail world for freedom into the beyond, examining for the thousandth time the same old bars that hemmed it in.

Etaoin moved jerkily, startling the serpent. It faced him, vibrating its tail against the wooden floor of its cage so that a whirring arose like a woodsaw's song.

THE SNAKE: Why do you stand there staring at me? You and I have nothing in common except our hatred of each other.

ETAOIN: You fascinate me. But why do you buzz your tail that way, mimicking a rattlesnake?

THE SNAKE: Why not? It is my fondest atavism.

ETAOIN: Could it be that the instinctive urge which prompts me to seek a tree when a dog barks at me is the same one that prompts you to endeavor to rattle when you are alarmed?

THE SNAKE: No. Your urge is born of fear. Mine of hate. Your instinct is one of cowardice. Mine one of counter-attack. You wish to flee. I to fight back. You are afraid of your own shadow. I am afraid of nothing.

ETAOIN: The god who gave you bravery gave me cunning.

THE SNAKE: I would not trade with you.

ETAOIN: Nevertheless, you are in a cage, and I am free to walk about.

THE SNAKE: Oh, you have your cage, too. You test your bars just as often as I test mine.

ETAOIN: I understand you somewhat vaguely.

THE SNAKE: I shall not be more explicit.

ETAOIN: Why do you keep rubbing your chin against the floor?

THE SNAKE: Why do you stand there like a fool? I do it because I like the sensation; because the friction gives me sensual pleasure; because my face itches and the rubbing ameliorates the irritation. Hah! Would you call scratching a counter-irritant for itching? Have I made an epigram?

ETAOIN: I doubt it.

THE SNAKE: Why do you wear those things over your eyes?

ETAOIN: In order to see.

THE SNAKE: The god that made you cunning made my eyes efficient enough to perceive objects without aid. In fact, the Lord of All Living dealt with me quite generously. Strength He gave me, and symmetry and endurance and patience. Viper and constrictor both He made me. My venom is more virulent than a cobra's. My coils are more terrible than a python's. I can slay with a single bite. I can kill with a single squeeze. And when I squeeze and bite at the same time, death comes galloping, I tell you. Heh, heh, heh! But look at you! You even have to hang rags on yourself to protect your weak skin. You have to hang things in front of your eyes in order to see. Look at yourself. Heh, heh, heh! God did well by you, indeed.

ETAOIN: I concede I am not His most perfect vessel.

THE SNAKE: What do you eat?

ETAOIN: I enjoy a catholicity of taste. I eat grapes and pig's feet, snails and fishes, proteins and carbohydrates. Also I am fond of gooseliver.

THE SNAKE: I eat only meat and fish and fowl. Once I ate a little brown boy. Shall I tell you about that?

ETAOIN: If you wish.

THE SNAKE: Well, my geography is not good, but it was on an island somewhere in some ocean, and it took a long time to swim there, and I swim fast. Notice how my tail is paddle-shaped. Well, I arrived at this island towards dawn of the seventh day; and there I decided to change my skin. It should have been changed days before, but one can't moult in mid-ocean. So I landed on a pretty little beach, steering through some treacherous rocks and breakers and only barely avoiding a dangerous stretch of shoal water. Out on the sand I glided, all eighty feet of me—at least, that is my length according to Doctor Lao, and he understands such matters—and I headed for some thick, trashy bushes I saw up on the bank a way. I tell you it is a bother to crawl about on land after swimming in the ocean. Well, I got in amongst the trashy bushes, sloughed and plowed my head around, and finally unhooked the epidermis from my upper and lower jaws. Then I snagged the ends of the old hide onto the bushes, and after that it was merely routine stuff wriggling out of the rest of it. The old skin bunches up under one's throat, you know, and gradually works back down off the rest of the body; and the faster you shag around in the bushes, the faster the old hide comes off. Well, I chased around and around, and off it came, and I was glad to see the last of it; it had become very uncomfortable the last day or so.

Now I have observed that every time I change my skin, immediately after the shedding I become hungry. So, gleaming and glistening and shining and sparkling and sleek and colorful in my new skin, I started looking about the island for something to eat. I went over a hill and through a forest and across a valley and never saw anything at all. Then I came to a river and swam up into the current. And it was a small river and a wiggly one, and when I would look behind me, all I could see would be myself disappearing around some bend. Well, I went up that river; and I tell you, all the little fishes in it thought their millennium had come.

Pretty soon I came to a town, a town of mud shacks and darky people. They were all loafing around near the river bank, listening to one of their medicine men tell what I doubt not was a most atrocious lie. I came sluicing up near them; they screamed and fled, and like chickens they fled in circles; and though you may not believe it, some of them actually hopped in the river and tried to swim across.

And I watched them and looked them over and picked out the one I wanted for a meal. I chose a little coffee-colored fat boy. Ah, I'll wager his mother had fed him on duck eggs and roast bananas he was so fat. Why, his belly rolled out so far he couldn't see his own knees.

Anyway, he chose to climb a tree. You know how those natives climb trees: tie their hind feet together and go up a slanting trunk with silly froghops. That's what this brat did. I let him get clear to the top, up among the fronds and coconuts. He looked down at me like a monkey, and the way he bawled one would have thought something terrible was about to happen to him.

Well, sir, I reaches up real easy-like, you know, easing up along the trunk, slow, slow; my hide rippling and undulating, as with soft efforts I give my head more altitude. And my old tongue what scares folks so—for they think it's a stinger—well, sir, my old tongue was just in and out all the time, giving it hell, I tell you. Gawd! I thought that lil nigger would bust his voice box when he seen my old tongue a-lickin' up at him, giving it hell thataway.

Well, sir, I snags him by the leg; an', Jesus, did he bawl then! But I gets a good holt, an' I says between my teeth: "Come outa that, you lil bastard!" an' I gives one hell of a yank; and, boyoboy, he lets loose, and I sways way back with him in my mouth and loses my balance, and we come crashing down to the ground with a hell of a jar. Damned near knocked me cold.

I swallowed him much as you would swallow an oyster and with every bit of as much right, if you will pardon an ethical intrusion. And just when he was well down between my jaws, so that my head was all swelled out of shape and my eyes were bugging out like lamp globes, why, damn me, if the kid's old pappy didn't come along with his fish spear and start to make trouble. Well, I couldn't do a hell of a lot of biting with the boy wedged in my mouth that way, but, believe me, fellah, I took care of the old man, all right. I got a hitch around him and his goddam fish spear with about the last third of my body; and when I got through squeezing him, he was ready to cry uncle, only he couldn't on account of his lungs being collapsed.

ETAOIN: You tell a vivid tale. What happened to the child's father?

THE SNAKE: Oh, I et him, too. And I looked around for the old lady, but I couldn't find her, so I just et the first vahine I came acrost. But the little fat boy was the best.

ETAOIN: You are a rare raconteur. Tell me of other of your meals.

THE SNAKE: No. It's your turn now. You tell me a story.

ETAOIN: There was a pig. A Duroc Jersey pig. It scampered about in its sty, eating slop and entertaining no spiritual conflicts. Fat it grew and fatter. Then one day its master loaded it into a wagon, took it to the depot, put it in a freight train, and sent it to a packing company. There it was slain, gralloched, and quartered after the manner of slaughterhouses. Some months later I went into a restaurant and ordered pork chops. And the chops they served me—may I die this instant if I lie—were from that very pig of which I have been talking. And the moral of this story is that the whole, sole, one and only and entire purpose of that pig's life, and the lives of its ancestors, and the lives of the things upon which pig and ancestors fed, and the climate and habitat that fostered their propagation and maturations, and the men who bred them and tended them and marketed them—the sole purpose of all that intermixed mass of threads and careers, I say—was to provide for me in that restaurant, at the moment I wanted them, a pair of savory pork chops.

THE SNAKE: There is merit in your contention. I philosophized along much the same lines when I was eating the little brown boy. Ah, I do so dearly love to talk about eating.

ETAOIN: There is but one subject more interesting.

THE SNAKE: I assume you refer to love.

ETAOIN: Yes. I do. Yes.

THE SNAKE: I still remember my first affair. It must have been eleven centuries ago. Ah, but she was lovely! Some twenty feet longer than I she must have been, for I was a yearling then; and her great fangs were like the blades of pickaxes. I was in the west; she was in the east. I smelled her all the way across the world. It was the first time I had ever smelled that smell, but I knew what it meant: funny how one knows some things without ever being told. I steered through the ocean waters to the east where she dwelled.

ETAOIN: It must have been a great voyage.

THE SNAKE: It was. I saw the nautilus, the squid, the obelia, and the elasmobranch shark. Flying fish flew about my head, and a frigate bird sailed over me. Hungry, I snatched the frigate out of the air and devoured it without even missing a stroke of my tail.

ETAOIN: How did it taste?

THE SNAKE: Nasty and fishy. I never ate another one. Pelicans, however, are not bad, and snow geese are extremely palatable.

ETAOIN: Well, did you find your mate?

THE SNAKE: Aye. Up alongside a brown rock island. She was cold and coy. She slithered up on top of the rocks and hissed at me. I slithered after her; my passion warmed her; my ardor allayed her coyness. Tell me, do men bite women on the neck when they woo them?

ETAOIN: Sometimes.

THE SNAKE: So do we. I bit her in the neck, and she hooked onto my lower jaw, and I could feel her poison circulate into me. But it didn't hurt me any; nor did mine hurt her. Then I dragged her off that rocky island, threw a loop or two about her, and so we wrestled in the bouncing, nervous waves. I remember the sky clouded and thunder muttered, as though the elements were disturbed by our antics. Tell me, do men tire of women after they have lain with them?

ETAOIN: Sometimes:

THE SNAKE: So do we. I tired and left her and returned to the west, to a place of enormous turtles and volcanic stones. The turtles there eat only vegetables and fruits; they attain tremendous age; and though they have never been elsewhere than their little volcanic island, they are profoundly wise. I lay in the sand and talked to to them. They asked me questions, and they told me many strange and beautiful things. Their feet are like the feet of elephants, and their voices slow and low. But tell me, after the period of surfeit wears off, do men again lust after women?

ETAOIN: Sometimes.

THE SNAKE: So do we. The following year I smelled her again, clear across the world again, too; and I heeded the call and went to her. And I went to her every year thereafter until . . .

ETAOIN: Until what?

THE SNAKE: Until Doctor Lao caught me and penned me up. Tell me, do men in cages . . . ?

ETAOIN: Sometimes.

THE SNAKE: So do we.

ETAOIN: People every now and again throughout maritime history have claimed to have seen you. Did you make a practice of sticking your head out of the waves and frightening people?

THE SNAKE: Oh, sometimes when I saw a boat, I'd swim over to it and look in it just for the fun of hearing the folks scream. I like to keep alive my legend, too, you know.

ETAOIN: Tell me how Doctor Lao managed to capture you.

THE SNAKE: It was on account of the mermaid. I had never seen anything like her before. Tell me, is she beautiful?

ETAOIN: Extremely so.

THE SNAKE: Well, I was puttering around off the China coast one day when Doctor Lao came along in his big old junk. The thing sailed right over me, as I was submerged at the time looking for cuttlefish. Directly, however, I came to the top to get some air, and I saw the doctor dragging what I took to be a big bright fish out of the water. He and all the coolies with him were yelling to beat the devil, so I swam up alongside to see what they had caught that excited them so. It was the mermaid. I just hung my head over the prow of that junk and stared at her. Then, while I was still in my trance, Doctor Lao threw a hawser loop about my neck and took a bight around the windlass with the other end. Just like a goddam rope, those Chinks hauled me up on deck. The damn hawser choked me unconscious, and when I came to I was in a cage. I've been in one ever since. That was nine years ago. But my day is coming. I don't forget.

ETAOIN: What will you do?

THE SNAKE: I shall dine, and Doctor Lao will furnish the meat course.

ETAOIN: Contingent, of course, upon your escape from this cage.

THE SNAKE: Exactly.

ETAOIN: After the meal, then what?

THE SNAKE: Oh, I shall get the mermaid, load her on my back—I think she can hold on if she uses her hands and fishtail at the same time—and then I shall get into the nearest river and swim to the sea. And nothing better try to stop me, either.

ETAOIN: Why take the mermaid?

THE SNAKE: She is a daughter of the sea just as I am a son of it. She yearns for it as much as I do. Besides, she is beautiful. You said so yourself. I will take her to the sea and free her there. Do you suppose she will wave her hand at me when she gets out into the tide? Do you suppose she will smile at me as she swims away?

ETAOIN: Of course she will.

THE SNAKE: I hope so. Then I will get upon the tide myself and go east to that brown, rocky island. My mate will still be there; I know she will. I shall go east to her. Obelia and nautilus and squid and elasmobranch shark—I shall see them all again.

ETAOIN: I'd like to go with you.

Mr. Etaoin wandered through the circus grounds waiting for the main performance to open. He encountered the lady reporter from the *Tribune* coming out of another tent.

"I'll bet you envy me," she said. "I've just had an interview with Doctor Lao himself!"

"Piffle," said Etaoin. "I've just had an interview with his snake."

Pleasantly saturated with Harry Martinez's good beer, Larry Kamper and his companion sat at the bar conversing and sipping and smoking. They had found interest and friendship each in the other, and had watered the seeds of their camaraderie with plentiful drenches of cool, mellow beer. Weather, hard times, and the parade having been talked out thin, the matter of Larry's career in the Orient in the service of his country's flag was now attacked.

"Man and boy," said Larry, "I put in six goddam years among the heathen and I come home to get civilized all over again. Jees, I was like a little farmer kid in a city fer the first time when I got to Frisco."

"Whereabouts was you in China, Larry?"

"Up in Tientsin most of the time. That's where the Fifteenth is stationed. Course we did a lot of chasing around, too."

"Wot kinda beer they got over there?" asked Harry Martinez.

"Oh, Asahi an' Sakura an' Gold Bottle an' Five Star an' Kupper an' Chess an' Spatenbrau an' Munchen an' a hell of a lot of other kinds. The Kupper was the best, though. Gawd, I drunk enough of it to float a battleship. Sure was fine beer."

"Well, wot kinda women was there?"

"Oh, there was all kinds—Koreans an Manchurians an' Japs an' Russians an' Cantonese an' Annamites an' Jews an' Latvians an' Slavs an' French an' Alsatians an' Filipinos. Hell of a lot of women. The Manchurians was the best, though. Big old cowlike girls with soft eyes an' big feet what they didn't never bind. They wore trousers an' jackets like men; and their hair was like black smoke, black, greasy smoke."

"I always heard," said his friend, "that them Chinese women was made different. Is that a fack?"

"Nah," said Larry, "they're just like any other women. Funny thing, though, a lot of Chink men think the same thing about white women. Wonder how that damn idea started, anyhow?"

Neither his friend nor Harry Martinez could help him in his bewilderment.

"Lord God," Larry's friend said, "I sure would like to travel around over the world and see funny people and queer places like you have. I all time wanted to travel, but I never will, I reckon; I'll just stick here in Abalone with the wife an' the kids and scratch along till I die. I was just thinking the other day why couldn't I slip off an' beat my way to the coast an' stow away on a boat goin' to Australia, maybe; anywhere so long as it was a hell of a ways off. And when I got there I could change my name an' start in all over again an' maybe have some fun some more. But I reckon I'll just stay here in Abalone with the wife an' kids till I rot."

"Ever see 'em do any beheading over there, Larry?" asked Harry Martinez.

"Oh, sure. Back in '27 they done a lot of it when the bandits got so bad. Us guys used to go to the native city every time there'd be an execution an' take pictures of the goddam thing. I got some good ones in my trunk what's in hock back in Frisco.

"One time down at a burg called Tongshan where we were doing guard while a revolution was going on, the Chink soldiers rounded up a bunch of deserters an' took a notion to have a public killing. They staged it in a rock quarry, an' all us guys went down to watch.

"They shot 'em that time instead of using the big knife. They'd take a guy out an' make him kneel down, an' then one of the Chink non-coms would come up with a big Mauser pistol an' let him have it between the horns.

"There was a hell of a big crowd of people standing around watching. Looking at executions was about the only thing there was to do in Tongshan anyway, except dig coal.

"Well, the Chinks they haul out the last guy, a great big bozo, an' fixes to bump him off an' call it a day. The non-com he snaps back the slide of his Mauser an' sees he's got a live shell in the chamber, an' then he steps over to plug the big boy. Well, the big guy he's awful nervous, an' he watches that Mauser out of the corner of his eye, an' just about the time the non-com pulls the trigger, the big boy jerks his head to one side, an' the non-com misses. It was the first time he'd missed a shot all day, too.

"But that doggone Mauser bullet it wanted blood, an' it hits a flat rock an' ricochets up into the crowd of on-lookers an' smacks a little kid right in the temple an' drops him in his tracks.

"An', damn me, if them Chinks didn't think that was a hell of a good joke. Why, they laughed an' laughed till they like to bust a gut. Sure are screwy people."

"I seen Pancho Villa 'dobe wall a bunch of guys once," said Harry Martinez. "But there didn't nobody laugh."

"Well, sir, the Chinese are a great outfit, all right," said Larry. "I kinda like 'em at that. Hey! Aint that circus run by a Chink?"

"Yeah."

"Well, come on; lets go. It oughtta be good."

All the way down Main Street Larry kept shuffling his feet, trying to keep step with his companion.

"Look at this damn town," mourned his friend. "I been stuck here since nineteen nineteen. Come here for the wife's health, an' I reckon I'll always be stuck here. Good Gawd! The rest of my life in Abalone. Damn place was dead when I got here, an' it's been getting deader. You been to China an' Japan an' the Philippines an' all them places, but I aint been nowhere 'cept Abalone, Arizona. Good Gawd!"

"Yeah, it's tough, all right," said Larry.

"What are you figgering on doing, Larry, when you pull out of this place?"

"Oh, I reckon I'll hunt up a recruiting station somewhere and enlist for the 11th Engineers in Panama. That's supposed to be a good outfit, an' it'll be a change from the infantry at any rate. After I get done with that hitch, I reckon I'll try the coast artillery in Hawaii, an' after that the air corps in the Islands, an' then maybe I'll go back to China. I dunno; there's a hell of a lot of places I want to see yet."

"You don't believe in settlin' down in one spot, do you?"

"Hell, no! I never did see the layout I didn't get sick of inside of a few years. That's the good thing about the army. When yer time's up you can get to hell out an' go somewhere else. 'Taint like holdin' down a civilian job."

"No," said his friend, "by God, I'll say it aint!"

They reached the circus grounds just as the two college youths landed on their ears in the middle of Main Street. Larry and his friend went over and helped them up.

"What's the matter, boys; get bounced?"

"Something of the sort," said Paul Conrad. "No matter; it's a lousy circus, anyway." He and Slick climbed into their old automobile, ground on the starter awhile and then swept away. On the back of the car was a painted legend:

FLAMING YOUTH . . . MIND OUR SMOKE

"Great guys, them college punks," said Larry admiringly. "They don't give a damn about nothin'."

People laughed when Doctor Lao went up to Larry Kamper and addressed him in Chinese, but their laughs turned to stupefaction when Larry replied in the vowelfluid music of High Mandarin. He sang the four-tone monosyllables as shrilly as did the doctor, and they talked as talk two strangers finding themselves in a foreign land with the bridge of a common language between them.

Their talking done, the doctor and Larry bowed and scraped and parted. And Larry went over to his friend and said: "Come on, the doc tipped me off to something hot. It's in this tent over here. Come on, you been wanting to see things. This ought to satisfy you."

They scuttled into a little dark tent. The doctor was already there. In a low cage a great grey bitch wolf whined and belched.

"I can't understand how it happened," said Doctor Lao. "Usually she's so regular about her periods. She wasn't due until October. Now right here in the middle of the circus she has to metamorphose. The equinox has something to do with it, I'm sure."

"Wot's he talking about?" whispered Larry's friend.

"The doggone old wolf's gonna change into a gal," said Larry. "Watch her; you never seen anything like it before, I'll bet."

"Aw, hell," said the man; "wotcha trying to feed me?"

"I aint feeding you nothing," protested Larry. "Aint you ever heard of werewolves? They change all the time. This here's one, an' she's fixing to change any minute now. Gawd, listen to her groan!"

"Well, I won't believe it till I see it," said the man. "An' then I dunno whether I'll believe it or not."

The wolf's guard coat, inturning, slipped under her wool. Across her belly her dugs marched, uniting as fat twins. Her canines blunted and recessed. Her tail shrunk.

"By gosh, something is happening to her," agreed Larry's friend. "Wotsa matter; is she sick?"

"No, no," said Doctor Lao, "just the usual preliminaries. Directly, you'll see her hind legs undergo drastic elongation. After that she changes very rapidly. Interesting, if you are interested in mutable morphology."

The wolf voiced sounds of agony, but not the sounds wolves customarily voice.

"You see," said Doctor Lao, "when a pollywog, for instance, metamorphoses into a frog, it is a long-drawn-out process, and any physical pain attendant to the change is counteracted by the very slowness of it all. But when a wolf changes into a woman, she does it in a very few minutes, and, hence, the pain is perceptibly intensified. Notice that as she changes she flits through the semblance

of every animal figure that forms a link in the evolutionary chain between hers and the human form. I often think
that the phenomenon of lycanthropy is nothing more than
an inversion of the evolutionary laws, anyway."

There was a gasp and a moan and a sob, and a woman
lay shuddering in the cage.

"Aw, doc!" said Larry in disgust, "why didn't you tell
us she was going to be so goddam old? Jees! That old
dame's like somebody's great-grandmother. Hell, I
thought we was going to see a chicken. Fer crying out
loud, put some clothes on her quick!"

"Sensualist," said the doctor. "I might have known your
only interest in this would be carnal. You have seen a
miracle, by any standard sacred or profane, but you are
disappointed because it gives no fillip to your lubricity."

"I'm a soldier, not a scientist," said Larry. "I thought
I was going to see something hot. How old's that old girl,
anyway—a hundred?"

"Her age is about three hundred years," said the doctor.
"Werewolves command a remarkable longevity."

"A three-hundred-year-old woman! Wow! An' I
thought I was going to see a chicken. Gawd, let's go pal."

Sonorously the great bronze gong banged and rang;
and from all over the circus ground the people, red and
black and white, left the little sideshow tents and shuffled
through the dust. The midway was thick with them for
a minute or two as they crowded toward the big tent.
Then the midway was desolate, save for its wreath of
dust, as the people all disappeared beneath the canvas. And
the ringing of the bronze gong diminuendoed and died.

The big tent was a dull creamy lacquer within. Black
swastikas were painted on it and winged serpents and fish
eyes. There were no circus rings. In the center of the
floor was a big triangle instead, a pedestal adorning each
angle. Doctor Lao, in full showman's dress of tails and
high hat and cracking whip, attained the top of one of
the pedestals and blew on a whistle. At a far entrance
a seething and a rustling was heard. Chinese music, mon-

otonous as bagpiping, teetled through the tent. Figures could be seen massing at the far entrance. The grand march was starting. The main performance had begun.

Snorting and damping, the unicorn came leading the grand march. Its hoofs had been gilded and its mane combed.

"Notice it!" screamed Doctor Lao. "Notice the unicorn. The giraffe is the only antlered animal that does not shed its antlers. The pronghorn antelope is the only horned animal that sheds its horns. Unique they are among the deciduous beasts. But what of the unicorn? Is it not unique? A horn is hair; an antler is bone; but that thing on the unicorn's head is metal. Think that over, will you?"

Then came the sphinx, ponderous and stately, shaking its curls.

"Say something to them!" hissed Majordomo Lao.

"What walks on four legs, two legs, three legs?" simpered the androgyne.

Mumbo Jumbo and his retinue came. The satyr syrinxed. The nymphs danced. The sea serpent coiled and glided. Fluttering its wings, the chimera filled the tent with smoke. Two shepherdesses drove their sheep. A thing that looked like a bear carried the kiss-blowing mermaid in its arms. The hound of the hedges barked and played. Apollonius cast rose petals. Her eyes blindfolded, her snakes awrithe, the medusa was led by the faun. Cheeping, the roc chick gamboled. On the golden ass an old woman rode. A two-headed turtle, unable to make up either of its minds, wandered vaguely. It was the damnedest collection Abalone, Arizona, had ever seen.

Mr. Etaoin, sitting behind Larry Kamper, said to Miss Agnes Birdsong: "Well, that's the whole outfit, I guess, except for the werewolf. I wonder where it is?"

Larry turned around. "See that old woman on the donkey's back? There's yer goddam werewolf."

Round and round the great triangle the animals walked, danced, pranced, fluttered, and crawled, Master of Ceremonies Lao directing them from his pedestal. They roared and screamed and coughed; rising from strings and reeds the Chinese music teetled monotonously and waveringly whined. Too close upon the fastidious unicorn, the sphinx accidentally nuzzled its rump; and the unicorn exploded with a tremendous kick, crashing its heels into the sphinx's side. The hermaphrodite shrieked. With its great paws it struck and roweled the unicorn's neck and back. The unicorn leaped like a mad stallion, whirled and centered its horn in the sphinx's lungs. Nervous, the chimera dodged about, its flapping wings fanning up dust clouds. The sea serpent reared into a giant S, launched a fifty-foot strike, caught the chimera by a forefoot, and flung seven loops about its wings and shoulders. The hound of the hedges curled in a tight ball, looking like a stray grass hummock. The Russian passionately kissed the mermaid. Lowering his horns, taking a short run for it, the satyr spiked Mumbo Jumbo in the rump when the black god's back was turned. The old woman changed back into a wolf and ravened at the roc chick. The little faun threw stones at Doctor Lao. The nymphs and shepherdesses and lambs hid and whimpered. From the face of the medusa the blindfold fell; eleven people turned to stone.

"Oh, misery!" screamed the doctor. "Why do they have to fight so when there is nothing to fight about? They are as stupid as humans. Stop them, Apollonius, quickly, before someone gets hurt!"

The thaumaturge hurled spell after spell among the hysterical beasts. Spells of peace, mediation, rationality, arbitration, and calmness flashed through the feverish air and fell like soft webs about the battlers. The din lessened. Withdrawing his horn from the sphinx's lungs, the unicorn trotted away and cropped at sparse grass. The sphinx licked at its lacerated side. The sea serpent loosed the chimera, yawned his jaws back into place. Shaking itself, the hound of the hedges arose and whined. The mermaid patted the bear. Mumbo Jumbo forgave the satyr. The werewolf remetamorphosed. The faun stopped throwing rocks. Back came the nymphs and shepherdesses and lambs. Once again the medusa assumed her blindfold.

After the storm, tranquillity. Peace and battle. Forgiveness and hate. The animals stood idle, panting, caressing their traumatized flesh. But in the eyes of one the heat of combat still burned. Blazing in its body, the lust to kill still flared; and the great snake coiled suddenly, struck like a catapult, and snatched Doctor Lao from his perch. All the way across the triangle the snake struck, nor could the eye follow the lightning flash of his head.

"Ah, my old implacable enemy!" gasped the doctor. "Only you would never become tame. Only you could never forgive. Help me, Apollonius, quick, lest he slay me!"

About the serpent the mage sent a haze of coldness; as the frost bit into the reptile's skin, its writhings slowed and its hot eyes glazed. Colder, colder, colder grew the haze; and the great snake grew sluggish as his blood thickened in the icy air. At length he lay still, a great grey ribbon, seeing but perceiving not, quiescent; rage still twisting his coils, but frozenly, not actively, twisting them.

Doctor Lao crawled away. "Keep him chilly until we get him back in his cage," he ordered. "Luckily I am immune to his poison. But he is treacherous and vindictive. I should have known better than to have let him out."

The show went on.

All others withdrawing, the sphinx was left in the triangle to perform solo—an acrobatic dance. Flinging tail, rump, hind feet into the air, it waltzed and schottisched and morrised on its forepaws, keeping time to indifferent dance music. Elegantly it curtsied upside down, dancing clumsily, humming and grinning.

"Ef it's gonna dance it oughtta have a partner," said someone.

"Heh, heh," laughed a quarantine inspector. "That there animal don't need no partner, does it, Al?"

"Nope," said Al. "It's Pierrot and Columbine all at the same time, by golly."

A huge boar trotted into the triangle.

"This is one you all haven't seen before," yelled the Chinaman. "The Gadarene swine itself. Fiend-infested, it searches the earth for salvation, but finds it not. Biblical beast, it symbolizes the uncleanliness of all flesh. Hence, sacramental butchery—to drive out latent devils; that is the purpose of the mummery of the priest-butchers."

Grunting and mumbling, the boar stopped to root. Out of its ear popped the head and shoulders of the devil that infested it. The little beelzebub waved his trident at Doctor Lao. "It's hotter than hell in this tent," he said.

"You ought to know," submitted the doctor.

The little ass of gold came forth. Ass and boar tripped a minuet.

"Why in the world," asked Mrs. Howard T. Cassan, "is it that everything in this circus dances all the time? I never saw anything like it."

"It's the dance of life, madam," said the old-like party in the golf pants. "You'll find plenty of precedent for it, if you look far enough."

The triangle cleared. Doctor Lao whistled; the hound of the hedges trotted out. It walked on its hind legs and flipped to its forelegs. It played dead and counted with laconic barks. Doctor Lao flung it lettuce leaves as a reward.

"Hell, I've seen better trained dogs than that'n," commented one of the policemen.

"So've I, mother," whispered Alice Rogers.

"Mother thinks it's very smart, Alice," said Mrs. Rogers, frowning at the cop.

"Why aint they got no elephants?" Edna Rogers wanted to know.

"Now, Edna, don't say 'aint,'" said mama.

"Well, I like tuh see elephants grab each other's tails," said Edna.

Mrs. Rogers said: "Oh, children, watch the funny bird. Look, it's so comical."

Imperfectly trained, the baby roc was walking a tight-rope. It lacked balance and grace, but in its talons it commanded a terrific grip, and it walked the rope as one would walk on vises instead of feet. Doctor Lao flung it hunks of ham as it reached the end of the rope. Snatching at the hocks and shreds, the chick fell forward; but its feet hung on and, describing a flapping half-circle, the roc swung over and hung head down from the rope. Nor would it let go. Doctor Lao gave it another bit of ham and tempted it with others to loosen its grip, but the huge red clumsy feet, bulging like knots around the rope, stuck fast. The upsidedown fledgling wept at its topsy-turviness and pleaded for more meat. Its thin-feathered wings drooped dismally; its great red-rimmed eyes regarded fearfully the sawdust in the triangle.

"Well, let go, you fool," stormed the doctor, "and we'll put you back in your nest. . . . I ask your forgiveness, good people; the unmanageableness of this incorrigible bird has spoiled the act."

"Give it a fishin' worm, doc," somebody suggested.

"Good heavens, man!" said the doctor, "rocs are raptorial birds, not vermivorous. They won't touch angleworms."

Mumbo Jumbo came from the dressing room, his tremendous blackness bringing a touch of color to the bareness. In one hand he carried a machete. With the other hand he grasped the tightrope. With the machete he hacked the rope in twain. The roc fell on its face. Mumbo Jumbo picked it up like a turkey and carried the squawking thing out of the tent.

"And now, ladies and gentlemen," said Doctor Lao, "it gives me great pleasure to announce that Apollonius of Tyana, greatest magician of all the world, will present to you his conception of the Witches' Sabbath. . . . Apollonius of Tyana . . ."

Catcalling "Louder and funnier!" from somebody in the unreserved section.

"Did them damn college punks slip back in?" asked Al.

"Apollonius of Tyana," repeated the ringmaster.

All in black, drowned in thought, the mage walked slowly to the triangle, waving away the murmur of applause.

Raising his hands, the left pointing straight up, the

right pointing straight down, he intoned sombrely: "Let there be darkness."

And a pall of darkness came into the tent, opaque and not to be seen through; and it crept into every angle and corner of the tent, so that one could not tell beside whom one sat; and even lovers had to touch and fondle each other in that darkness for reassurance.

"Moonlight," commanded the mage. "Moonlight. Soft music on the piccolo."

Into the black pall crept a beam of moon silver, furtive and uneasy, as though it felt it did not belong there, and soft music on the piccolo accompanied its creeping. And the moonlight spread and illuminated a meadow, in the center of which was a pig-wallow, fat with mud, thin with water. Idle weeds grew all about with thislets and ragspurs among them; and from the thin water of the wallow came the high concupiscent minstrelsy of the frogs singing their frantic nuptial songs. Brighter turned the waters of the wallow, till the wallow became a disk of moonbeams, a dishful of lambency. Eyes gleamed in the water; fish eyes, toad eyes and frog eyes, salamander eyes, turtle eyes, and crustacean eyes. They palpitated in the moonbeams.

Scurrying through the meadow came small animals: badgers, minks, and hedgehogs, squirrels, rats, and marmots, cats, stoats, and kit foxes. Their eyes made a circle of blue points as they amassed about the wallow. They knew not why they gathered there, but there they were from forest and fen and hill and hunt; and they all came and gathered there, nor did they bicker and squabble but gathered silently; and silently they waited, wondering why they waited, beside the pig-wallow in the moonlight.

In the thin water the turtles swam unceasingly, the keels of their shells rippling the water with soft swishes. And the salamander crawled out on the bank and into the water again, over and over; while the frogs stilled their love songs, ceased their egg-laying. A water moccasin seized a green bullfrog; the frog screamed his death scream in the moonlight. And all the other frogs moaned and huddled greenly under weed leaves.

"Silence!" roared Apollonius.

"The snakes attack us," whimpered the minstrels.

"Silence!" said the magician.

Then the witches came. Straight from the mountains of the moon they came, riding on their broomsticks down the highway of moonbeams to the pig-wallow and the waiting hosts. Lovely some, ugly others, thin and rancid, fat and nasty, old and youthful, repulsive and divine, they came and came. Some were ill from their rapid flight and vomited strange fluids, and some spat blood. Some were cowled like nuns. In lavish circles whirling, broomstick-borne, they skittered over the water top; weird women flying, their snarls and tatters streaming, laughing profanely like bawds; circling, circling, then alighting. The wallow banks blackened with the thronging of the sisters; sisters of temptation, sisters of falsehood, sisters of decay. A convocation of garrulous crow-women, unwashed, unshriven, undesirable, and sterile, they hopped about in the mud and cackled.

"Dance," said Apollonius. "The master cometh."

In the middle of the water, on the back of a huge turtle, a fire flared in an iron brazier. Firelight fought moonlight, and the moonlight died; and the gold of the firelight washed away from the wallow the silver of the moonlight. The batrachians, turtles, and salamanders raised their wet heads, marshaling like troops to form a living bridge to the fire. And the witches, raising their skirts, tripped out upon the water over the pathway of the water dwellers' heads. Ringaroundabout the flaring fire they danced.

Croaking, the frogs marked the measures of the steps. And bats came, night-borne, to greet the dancing sisters. Like wavering, restless flakes of soot the bats came; hovering about the witches' ears they squeaked at them; alighting in their hair they bit their ears with friendly bites and chided them and told them secret things.

From the brazier on the fire-bearing turtle a red-hot

flaming coal fell. Before it reached the water a toad, taking it for a brilliant bug, snapped it up with his agile tongue and swallowed it, and then writhed convulsively as its belly burned. And the great turtle, watching his flame, now and again drove his head down into the muck to bring up in his jaws shreds of peat and snags of wood to toss over his head into the flames and so replenish the fire. And as the wet dripping fuel fell into the flames a hissing would arise on wings of steam.

The stoats and minks loosened the drawstrings of their scent sacs; the viscous stinks flooded the pond air. And the tomcats yelled, their soprano voices higher and keener and in contrast to the bass belling of the bullfrogs. And the kit foxes barked. And the hedgehogs made uncomfortable, small squealing noises. The badgers sat on their haunches, watching, their masklike faces quizzical, their stripes awry, their coats damp and muddy.

And the witches whirled and danced and giggled and coughed and grimaced as the stink of the minks smote them. And the animals made their grotesque noises, singing the music for the dance.

"More vigor!" called the thaumaturge. "The master cometh!"

The animal calls increased; staccato, they crackled in the pond air. And the witches whirled the faster, danced the madder, while the fire sparkled, surged, and roared.

Then above the flames, bored, fat, over-sexed, nervous, smoking a cigarette, Satan Mekratrig appeared. Green he was, with black patches of mildew on his face and shoulders. He blew grey rings and studied the dancing.

"Terrible," he said. "Terrible. I never saw such terrible dancing. Pick it up! Pick it up!" And Satan snatched a whip out of the air and flogged the witches. With long lash snapping, the whip danced about the dancing sisters, the tongue of it swirling among them, slashing them and stinging them. And among them the whiplash lit the oftenest upon the youngest witch, a pale slender supple witch, a nude ivory dark-haired witch, Demisara, witch of incest, witch of shame. And the old burnt-out sisters were envious of this mark of favor; they jerked and hissed at her, and covertly they spat at her; but the whip of Satan lit ever and again on the young desirable shoulders of Demisara and curled about her waist and crackled over her back; and the shriveled old harridans sneered to see that Mekratrig had him a new favorite.

The animals all slipped into the water and joined the dance, wallowing through the mud, trampling down the crayfish, minnows, and tadpoles, leaping among the frogs. Hovering in his flame, Satan laughed at the careful bedraggled cats afraid of wetting their feet, afraid not to dance, loathing the water and the mud, and stepping about as on hot rocks. He grabbed hunks of flame from the fire and tossed them upon the water where they burned among the furry things, igniting coats, singeing whiskers, racing through tails. The animals bawled as they burned and scorched, but danced on and on and on.

And Satan Mekratrig reached over and caught Demisara by the hair and jerked her free of the other sisters and snatched her to him in the flames and loved her there. Starshine was in her eyes; drops of dew gleamed upon her shoulders.

"Better stop it, Apollonius," Doctor Lao warned, "or it will be getting out of hand in a minute."

"Moonlight!" called the mage. "Shrill music on the piccolo!"

With a rush the moonlight returned, blotting out the blaze of fire. The screeching of the piccolo drowned the noise of the animal calls. Satan Mekratrig howled out an oath; it lingered like blue smoke in the air. The rhythm of the dance wavered and broke. The visibility faded. The fire died. The animals disappeared. Back to the mountains of the moon streamed the witches on their broomsticks. And the moonlight crept away, and only the pall of darkness remained.

"Let there be light," commanded the magician.

Light came, the daylight of Abalone, Arizona, to illuminate the tent. But in the center of the tent above the tanbark, suspended in air, Satan Mekratrig still remained, and struggling in his arms was Demisara. The devil screamed at Apollonius, defying banishment. Froth formed on his lips from the vehemence of his screaming.

Reaching into his robe, the magician drew out a crucifix. Holding on high the little Jesus quartered on a cross, he advanced beneath the fiend. There was a burst of flame in the center of the tent, and witch and devil disappeared. Apollonius kissed and put away the artifact.

The applause was sparse and unconvincing. Apollonius and Doctor Lao bowed gravely to each other. Then, drowned in thought, the magician plodded back to his quarters.

Rapidly thereafter the animals went through the remaining portions of the repertory. Golden ass and hound of the hedges put on a dog and pony show. In purple tights and scarlet sash the satyr came grinning; with his sharp, sure horns he spiked balloons which Doctor Lao inflated and flung to him. Ungaubwa, the high priest of the Negroes, using one of the black girls for a target, threw knives and hatchets, pinning her by her clothing to a shield. From a high ladder the mermaid dived into a tiny tank. In gay Grecian robes the nymphs came, singing the Sirens' Song, the same song that Doctor Browne asserted was not difficult of divination but which, nevertheless, he did not hazard to name, contending himself merely with the claim he could do so any time he got around to it.

Shepherdesses and lambkins followed the Siren Song singers. They cavorted in an afternoon full of the fresh lissomeness of the time of May. Like figures on thin old chinaware were these shepherdesses and lambkins, almost as ideal, almost as tenuous. The audience relaxed drowsily while watching them. Then a cruel, bitter, black cloud came roaring from nowhere; and over the edge of the cloud the sweating face of Satan Mekratrig was thrust, greenly grinning down at the sweet shepherdesses and gamboling lambkins. And lambkins and shepherdesses shuddered and cringed.

"Oh, why does the symbol of evil come into everything and every scene in this circus?" cried Miss Agnes Birdsong. "That cynical old Chinaman, that's all he knows? There is purity and there is simplicity and there is goodness without any hint of bad about them. I know there is! Oh, he's wrong!"

"It's only a circus," said Mr. Etaoin. "Don't let it disturb you."

Doctor Lao heard her, too.

"The world is my idea," he said. "The world is my idea; as such I present it to you. I have my own set of weights and measures and my own table for computing values. You are privileged to have yours."

He waved away the shepherdesses and the fiend and the time of May. Climbing back on his pedestal, he announced:

"The afternoon grows late. On some of your faces I detect symptoms of an awful ennui. Well, there is but one more scene to this circus: it is the spectacle of the people of that ancient city Woldercan worshiping their god Yottle, who was the first and mightiest and least forgiving of all the gods.

"Piety such as theirs exists no more. Such simple, trusting faith is lost to the world. When you folks here in Abalone worship your god, I understand you do it in a church wired for sound, so that every pleasure automobile, radio-equipped, can, even at sixty miles an hour, hear you at your prayers. But does your god? Ah, well . . . what does it matter?

"For your better understanding of this Woldercan episode, it is necessary that I tell you Woldercan was in the midst of a drought. Rich and poor alike there had nothing to eat, for such was the dryness that nothing could grow. That was a calamity Woldercan had never before been called upon to face; for, while the poor had always been with them and chronically starving, after the fashion of the poor, theretofore the rich had always lived, after the custom of the rich, off the fat of the land. Yet now there was no food for anyone, not even the rich; nor could all the coin of the realm buy even a rotten turnip.

"Terror, the great leveler, swept into the city. The politicians could do nothing; the police could do nothing; the scholars could do nothing; the rich could do nothing. The people stood around in small fearful groups, waiting for death to come slowly via the route of starvation.

"But one man among them did something. That man was he who was the high priest of Yottle. He walked rapidly among them, and:

" 'Come,' he said. 'Gather in the temple. We will pray to Yottle. Yottle will protect his own.'

"So then all Woldercan, having naught else to do, went to Yottle's temple to pray.

"Now that episode of the starving Woldercanese, in Yottle's temple, praying to him for relief, is surely one of the great and vivid and dramatic scenes of all recorded history; and it is with pride that I bring it to you with my circus. As a little hint as to what happens, I want to recall to you that they sacrifice a virgin to their god. Piety. That was real piety. When you people here of Abalone pray to your god for a drought's end, do you go to such extremes in your protestations of faith? Would you sacrifice Abalone's fairest virgin? Ah, well . . ."

Then Doctor Lao left his pedestal and sidled away a little. He doffed his showman's hat. "Ladies and gentlemen," he called, "I give you Yottle's temple in ancient Woldercan!"

And the rear of the tent curled up and back, and there before the eyes of Abalone, Arizona, was the interior of the great somber towering temple of the great god Yottle. And, somber, too, the music of the spheres welled in rolls up from nave and chancel, lingered about the giant beams, and rose higher, ever higher, even to the gold bar of Heaven itself.

Above the altar on an ivory dais Yottle sat. One hand was upraised; the other caressed his throat. His eyes, peering from jeweled eyelids, contemplated things far off from earth. Incense pots smoked about his ankles. He was bigger than a mastodon, fleshier than a hippopotamus, and more terrifying than either. Bronze was Yottle's flesh, and his fat was a brazen fatness. In a coign beneath his dais rested his sacred stone ax, the sacrificial tool, the brutal mace of death.

The tattered, starveling Woldercanese, eleven thousand strong, were forlornly moaning piteously and some of them were chaunting low hymns of lost hope. Gray were the faces of the Woldercanese, and it was the grayness of hunger and the grayness of fear which tinted them.

Out of the gray mass the high priest arose; there was a sort of holy glowing about his head. He blessed them with his hands, and:

"Peace," he said. "Patience and peace."

Then the high priest turned to Yottle, making mystic, cabalistic signs.

He knelt. He prayed.

"Glory unto thy name, Yottle; homage before thy eyes, Yottle; Yottle the all-knowing, Yottle, the omnipotent. Sinners all, we come before thee, foul with the sins of sloth and greed and hate and lust. Weary, we cannot sin more. Surfeited, we sicken and are afraid. Despairing and ashamed, we turn to thee. Dying, we remember our forgotten prayers. Hopeless, we plead: Lord of our world, forgive us; Light of our gloom, enlighten us; Creator of the spheres, aid us; Yottle, great Yottle, forgive us now, forgive."

But one of the men stood up in the rear of the temple and protested:

"Why do you pray like that? We assuredly are not ashamed of ourselves. We are not foul with sin and lust. The only reason we are here at all is because Yottle has seen fit to withhold rain from our crops. We don't want forgiveness. We want rain and something to eat. Tell Yottle so. Your business is to intercede for us, not tattletale about us." He turned to the people.

"Am I not right?" he asked.

"You certainly are," they said. And to the priest they said: "Of course he is right. We have sinned; yes. But we are not entirely without virtue. In the next period of your prayer, minimize our bad points and accentuate our good ones. Don't make us out a troop of pindling sinners wading through a manure mire of our frailties. Tell Yottle of the straits we are in, if you like, but don't be so anxious to admit we merit them, because we don't believe we do."

Bitterly, the high priest answered them:

"So! You criticize me and humiliate me here before the very eyes of Yottle! You tell me, your high priest, how to pray! Very well."

He turned to Yottle, shouting:

"Hey, thou lump of bronze and shining stones! Look upon us and marvel that such magnificent people do not throw you down and melt you up and make trinkets of your metal. We do not fear. We are great. Woldercan does not petition; she ordains. Hear us and act:

"Food we must have immediately. And immediately, too, we must have rain that we may raise more food. So out of thy cosmic kitchen, Yottle, throw us down some pie from heaven, and with thy sprinkling pot wet down our dead grain fields. Feed us, Yottle, well and quickly; fill our——"

But before the priest could say more, a high keen passionate rush of words drowned out his own. And the words came from everywhere at once, as the hurricane comes; and flood-like the words came from all sides; then they ceased.

The Woldercanese fell down on their faces. That had been Yottle's voice, and they knew it.

The priest was the first to arise. With his hands he blessed them.

"Peace," he said to his flock. "Peace and fear nothing. Yottle has spoken. He is indignant, but he is willing to be mollified. He says he doubts our faith in him, but he is willing to put it to test. But he says he is so angry now that we must sacrifice our fairest virgin to him before we do anything else. He says sacrifice her first, then talk to him later about rain. He is very angry. He will not allow us much time. Haste is paramount, my children. So, quickly, let us sacrifice the virgin and appease him. Let us immediately placate our infuriated god."

"How are you going to find the fairest virgin, though?" demanded the man who had interrupted before.

"We will hold a beauty contest here and now," said the priest. "Let all our virgins line up; we will choose the loveliest by popular acclaim. It will be a great honor for her. Besides, it is better that only one should die than the whole populace. That is the theory of sacrifice. So let all the virgins line up here. Please, now! Quickness is essential. Yottle is very angry. Hurry! Hurry!"

A dozen girls formed a nervous row.

"Acgh!" said the priest in disgust, "there are more girls than this in Woldercan. I can see more with my own eyes. Come! Come!"

Some realist reminded him one of the specifications was on the count of true maidenhood.

"Gracious," said the priest. "Of course. That explains it. Very well. As I walk behind these girls, my children, and hold my hand over their respective heads, you will, by your applause, indicate the one you wish for the bride of Yottle."

Facing the faces of the people of Woldercan, the twelve lumps of ripe but untasted sex stood posing, stood waiting for the accolade that would bring to one of them the crown of beauty, the caress of death. The old trembly priest doddered behind the girls, holding over their fair, triumphant heads—fair with grace and charm, triumphant with youth and life—his wrinkled hands. And throbs in greater and lesser volumes of applause spread through the congregation as over each head in turn the priestly hands were questioningly poised. And over the twelfth head, a dark little, proud little, exquisite little head, as the aged hands were raised, the applause became thunderously loud, ever increasing, rising, and echoing; and the bride of Yottle had been chosen.

But from the throng there came a great choking cry. And the man who had interrupted the high priest's prayer knelt in sudden, sunken, awful misery. For Woldercan had chosen his sweetheart, his betrothed.

The priest consoled him ineffectually. "Yottle's ways

are not always to be understood, brother," he said. "And Yottle doubtless inspired the people to choose her. Peace, brother, and fear nothing. Glory awaits her."

The people were keyed to a tottering pitch. "Come!" they called. "Come. Never mind him. Let's have the sacrifice."

"Yes," said the priest. "Now bow your heads."

Acolytes in an honor guard hush-hushed the congregation as, a little behind them, the virgin walked to the altar. A strange dark light was on her face, and above her head a faint pallid halo hung. She was of Woldercan no more; they knew it. Staring at her with twisted, side glancing eyes, they wondered, now that she was consecrate, why they had not perceived her holiness before. And the temple of her flesh moved through the throng in the temple of Yottle, a sweeter, holier temple, more mysterious and provocative of a greater adoration than the stone temple through which she walked.

Her lover flung up his head pathetically, and he screamed tragically:

"Oh, stop her! Stop her! Good God Almighty, stop her! Let me die instead. Let us all die rather than let her even be touched. That brazen image; this lovely girl; kill the one to placate the other? Madness! Oh, hell and heaven, do not slay her for that idol!"

"Be still!" said the people. "Sit down! You are hysterical. Yottle has spoken and we will sacrifice her to him. Glory to Yottle's name! From him all wisdom stems and flowers. Do your duty, priest."

From the coign beneath the dais of ivory, the high priest lifted the sacred stone ax. He directed the virgin to unclothe herself that she might go to Yottle unhampered by linen and cotton coverings. The Woldercanese were shaking and roaring with excitement. The temple itself seemed to quiver.

The old priest expectorated in his thin palms and hoisted the ax.

Then did the lover spring up like a hind and dash through the multitude to the side of his loved one. Shrieking "No, no!" and "Stop, stop!" he grappled with the high priest, fighting furiously for the monolithic tool. The people of Woldercan bellowed ferociously as a fury fell upon them. It seemed that, mob-like, they would storm the altar.

But very quietly, yet with a horrid, impatient suddenness, Yottle fell forward off his ivory dais. His upraised hand caught the battling lover on the head, cracking it like a nut. Unable to escape, priest and virgin, too, were crushed by the fall of his great brazen body. There beneath the altar lay three corpses and the great god Yottle.

High from the fair heaven came loaves of manna, falling to the hungry Woldercanese. And for their crops a thin wispy rain came weeping into the wind, drizzling and dripping.

Then the ends of the tent fell outward and down, and the circus of Doctor Lao was over. And into the dust and the sunshine the people of Abalone went homewards or wherever else they were going.

THE CATALOGUE

(An explanation of the obvious
which must be read to be appreciated.)

1. The Male Characters

DOCTOR LAO: A Chinese.

MR. ETAOIN: A corrector of errors.

APOLLONIUS OF TYANA: A legend.

AN OLD-LIKE PARTY IN GOLF PANTS: A bore.

A QUARANTINE INSPECTOR: A good party man.

ANOTHER QUARANTINE INSPECTOR: A good party man.

ISKANDER: A legend.

ISKANDER'S CAPTAIN: Diogenes of Damos. An expert with a longbow; could hit an obolus three out of seventeen tries at nineteen paces.

KUBLAI KHAN: In his day he was China.

LUTHER: A voice, not a face; likewise a harried homunculus; likewise ultimately the owner of a fine statue.

A RAILROAD TRAFFIC OFFICER: Described in the text.

UNGAUBWA: A black priest, differing from that other black priest, Montanus, both as to creed and virility.

JOHN ROGERS: Learned the plumbing trade at fourteen, fifteen, sixteen, and seventeen. Never made a hell of a lot of money at it, however. A good union man.

PAUL CONRAD GORDON: His father was way up in the bond business back in Detroit. Paul majored in mechanical engineering but after he graduated got a job as an aluminum salesman. It paid more.

SLICK BROMIEZCHSKI: His old man was a Polish immigrant, but Slick was so hot at football in high school that one of the temples of higher education made it worth his while to keep on with his culture. Mentioned as all-

101

America end in some of the lesser sporting journals during his junior year.

CLOWNS: Pantaloons whose hearts are bursting.

CROWD OF MEXICANS LARRY KAMPER SHOULDERED HIS WAY THROUGH: Peons, agrarians, hacendados, padrones, prize-fighters, bullfighters, laborers.

BILL: William R. Johnston. He had been drinking the night before he saw the parade and didn't feel so good that morning. Shot a good game of golf.

BILL'S FRIEND: Murray R. Kaldwell. In the ready-to-wear business. A sound merchandise man and a good window-dresser. Didn't like at all the kind of ads Steele would lay out for him in the *Tribune*.

TEDDY ROOSEVELT: An American President.

A RUSSIAN.

HARVEY: Harvey R. Todd. When Frank Tull told him and Helen what he had seen at the circus, Harvey and Helen always regretted they hadn't gone.

A FAUN: See Praxiteles.

JOE: A voice, not a face. Tenor, but rasping.

FRANK TULL: Described in the text. A good man before a jury.

PETTY CHINESE PRINCES: Wang Wei, Wang Foo, Wang Goo, Wang Chow. Not even legends any more.

LARRY KAMPER: Described in the text. After he got to Panama, he got into trouble and stood special court-martial for violation of Article of War Number ninety-six. They sent him up for nine months in the guard-house, and while Larry was there he became awfully efficient at policing up around the post. Awfully nice chap, if you didn't expect too much of him. Good guy to go on a drunk with. The dirtier the story you told him, the louder he'd laugh. Old Larry didn't give a damn whether school kept or not and was the first to tell you so.

HARRY MARTINEZ: His forefathers came to this country a little after Hernando Cortez. His foremothers, May-ans, Toltecs, and Aztecs, were already here.

LARRY KAMPER'S FRIEND: Walter R. Dones. A truckdriver,

temporarily out of employment. He wasn't so good at spotting a truck, but he could keep one running, and that was more than most of the other guys could do.

POLICE FORCE OF ABALONE: Ex-cowpunchers, ex-railroad men, ex-bootleggers, ex-sheriffs, ex-contractors, ex-farmers. Mighty good policemen, too. Of course, they'd cut one another's throats now and then playing politics and all, but, hell, a guy's got to look out for himself these days. It's a goddam cinch no one else will.

"TRIBUNE" AD MANAGER: Everybody liked him, and those who were under him said he was the best boss they'd ever had.

STEELE: Just dumb enough so that most merchants would listen to him when he wanted to sell them a little display space.

"TRIBUNE" CITY EDITOR: An able man. Should have been on a better paper, but his health kept him in Abalone.

CHINESE TROOPS IN TONGSHAN, CHINA: Members of Chang Tsolin's Manchurian forces. Coolies dressed in scarecrow uniforms, handed guns they didn't know how to shoot, and dubbed soldiers. No pay. Rations, a couple of doughballs every day. None regretted he had only one life to give for China.

PANCHO VILLA: A legend.

THE DEAD MAN APOLLONIUS BROUGHT BACK TO LIFE: Arnold R. Todhunter. A homesteader. Later on, when a *Tribune* reporter interviewed him about the hours he spent in the arms of death, he testified he was just on the point of being issued a harp and a gown when Apollonius reclaimed his clay. He said Heaven reminded him more than anything else of an advertisement he had once read of Southern California.

A CONDEMNED CHINESE DESERTER: Lin Tin Ho. Age thirty. Survived by his wife and two daughters. A Shanhaikwan farmer. Impressed into the service on May 11. Shipped to Tongshan May 18. Deserted May 19. Captured May 20. Tried and sentenced May 21. Executed May 22. Pictures of his execution still may be purchased in Tientsin and Peiping. Lots of tourists and missionaries have them. The thing to do is buy one of those snapshots showing Lin getting pistoled, take it home with you carelessly intermixed with pictures of temples and canals, and then when your friends, who are looking over your Chinese album, run across it, why, just nonchalantly pass it off as a little thing you took yourself. There's no way to check on you, unless someone you show it to has seen it before.

RED, BLACK, AND WHITE PEOPLE OF ABALONE: American Indians such as Papagos, Pimas, Apaches, Yaquis, and Yumas. Aframericans such as quadroons, high yallers, octoroons, seal-skin browns, and mulattoes. Whites such as Spanish Americans, Texans, Easterners, Californians, and health-seekers and dude ranchers.

NEBULOUS PEOPLE SOME DAY TO BURY MRS. CASSAN: A minister, an undertaker, a gravedigger, some mourners, and some morbid curiosity-seekers.

NEBULOUS PEOPLE SOME DAY TO EXHUME FRANK TULL: A contractor, a straw boss, and seven laborers. They didn't do it on purpose. They were fixing to dig the holes for the foundation of a new T.B. sanatorium and didn't know they were scratching into sepulchral ground.

DOCTOR BROWNE: He found some pots in an arable field between Buxton and Brampton but belonging to Brampton; burial urns they were.

PHINEAS TAYLOR BARNUM: See his autobiography.

CIGARETTE FIENDS: Serfs of the narcotic lady nicotine.

GAUTAMA: Wherever he sat, ultimately a bo tree flourished.

GLASSBLOWERS: Artisans.

RESURRECTED SUPERMEN: Usually disappointments, for their legends have towered higher than they are able to reach.

DARK MEN IN MRS. CASSAN'S LIFE: Wops, Spicks, Frawgs, and furriners.

TURBANED MYSTIC: Swami. Yogi. Mahatma. Krishna.

UNSCRUPULOUS FINANCIERS AND POLITICIANS: Bankers, Aldermen.

HERMES: A legend.

CITY CLERK: A voice over the telephone.

MEN THAT STAYED OUT ON THE HILLS WITH THEIR FLOCKS: This was before the cattle-sheep feuds of the West. But, anyway, these men and their followers are largely responsible for the wealth of sheepherder stories that flood the world today. And where there is fire, there must be smoke. The Book of Leviticus contains many a specific warning, Godspoken to Moses, about the penalties of loving your live-stock unwisely and too well.

RAILROAD TRAFFIC OFFICER'S FELLOW-WORKER: Howard R. Ginter. He looked like he might be a prizefighter, but in reality he was just a bookkeeper. He made very good home brew.

ASTROLOGERS OF CHALDEA: Starwatchers.

GEOLOGIST FROM THE UNIVERSITY: Understood cleavages and erosion and, from a single jawbone, he could tell what the hind foot and the fundament of the beast were like.

ROUGH-LOOKING MEN WHO LOADED KATE ON THE TRUCK: Leslie R. Stevens, George R. Smith, Peter R. Summerton, and Claude R. Watson. They never did figure out just what the hell Kate was, but they complained to Luther that the thing was awful damn heavy.

FORGOTTEN EGYPTIAN TAXIDERMIST: Originally an embalmer of princes, hakims, bashas, chosroeses, and effendis, he extended his art to the preservation of dead animals. He knew about the circulation of blood long before Harvey did.

MONK FROM TIBET: He lived in a yurt, ate tea thick with butter, wondered a lot about life, took a vow of chastity but broke it when he was in Alexandria, discovered the Ovis poli and the spectacled bear, not knowing what he had discovered, knew some good jokes, and died without ever being really satisfied.

SIMPLE FOLK BY A LAKESIDE WHO SAW THE YOUNG SATYR: Greek agriculturists.

THE LITTLE FAT BROWN BOY'S FATHER: A spearer of fishes and a good husbandman. When he planted rice seeds rice came up. When he planted plantain seeds plantain came up. When he planted his own seed the little fat brown boy came up.

MASTER OF THE DUROC JERSEY PIG: James R. Sawyer, a small farmer in Missouri. If it hadn't been for his eyes seeing things and his belly wanting them, the money that he might have saved would have made a considerable pile.

THE CHINESE TRAVELER FROM THE NORTHERN CAPITAL: Liu Beaow. A scholar, but a secret apostate to the teachings of both Gautama and Con Fu Tze.

THE GUYS PANCHO VILLA 'DOBE-WALLED: There were two outstanding ones. One had been a notorious killer himself, and when he stood there facing the Villa rifles and looking at the sun and sky for the last time, he broke down and cried as no baby ever cried. The other was an unfortunate who had never killed anyone nor even hurt anyone, but he belonged to the wrong party. He faced the rifles with calmness and waved a good-by to his friends.

THE NOBODY THAT DIDN'T LAUGH WHEN PANCHO VILLA 'DOBE-WALLED THE GUYS: Harry Martinez, Felix Bustamante, Carlos Villalobos, Carlos Delgado, Michael Pierpont, Pierre Maeyer, Pancho Villa, the seven members of the firing squad, and the guys that got killed.

THE BELVEDERIAN DOCTOR: He taught his students that it was better to live a life rather than earn a living.

HIGH PRIEST OF YOTTLE: Converted to the faith at the age of forty-seven. Ordained at fifty-seven. Went on an evangelical mission which lasted seven years. Saved and baptized the heathen right and left. Succeeded to the high-priestship in his ninety-seventh year. Died steadfast in the faith.

MAN WHO INTERRUPTED THE HIGH PRIEST: A lowborn, argumentative, vulgar, deceitful fellow.

A REALIST IN WOLDERCAN: He had that sort of thing on his mind all the time.

II. The Female Characters

KATE: A sad memory.

THE RAILROAD MAN'S WIFE: Martha. Calm, sad, insecure; sometimes she laughed; laughing, she wondered; wondering, she wanted to cry.

MISS AGNES BIRDSONG: The boys all said she was damned good company after she learned to smoke and drink. Doctor Lao's circus broadened her outlook, gave her things to think about when sleepless she tossed on her couch of nights, when bored she listened to her pupils botch syntax of days.

MRS. HOWARD T. CASSAN: Described in the text.

THE WIFE OF PLUMBER ROGERS: Sarah. Loved her children, liked her husband, was content in Abalone, cooked good things to eat, kept a neat home, dreamed of no miracles, desired no victories, fretted when it was time to fret, laughed when it was time to laugh.

TWO SHEPHERDESSES: Dora Beaulais and Dulce Bonaventura.

A CHORUS OF NYMPHS: Dorothy, Louise, Hilda, Elsie, Laura, Opal, Eva. Dorothy, Isabel, Helen, and Hildegarde; Dorothy, Dorothy, Dorothy.

FIVE COLORED GIRLS: Quintet of pigmented maidens. Pigmented quintet of girls. Girlish quintet of pigmentation.

MRS. FRANK TULL: Before her marriage Valerie Jones. Frank was a disappointment to her. She was a disappointment to Frank. There were in her life other disappointments, too. For instance, Nature had not endowed her with all the lovely beauty she thought her due, so, in order to augment that little which she had, she covered herself with objects themselves lovely and beautiful, and strove through theirs to add to her lack. From tiny holes in her ears she hung gold and jeweled pendants. Into the pores of her cheeks she rubbed ointments and greases of suave colors. Over her legs she drew stockings of sheer silk. Around her wrists she placed gauds of silver and bright stones. Up her fingers

she slid little hoops of metal embossed with carbon.
Upon her lips she dabbed rouge. Her abdomen she up-
held with a belt and a corset. Her breasts she fitted into
pert pouches. Over her feet she laced tight little shoes.
Around her shoulders she flung animal skins. Her hair
she had permanently waved. Powder she put on her
neck and upon her throat; and under her arms, previously shaven smooth, she syringed a deodorant. Thus
she managed to change her color, her figure, and her
smell, and at the same time gleam with bright metal and
glossy fur and dull silk and brilliant stones. Yet, by
heaven, even then she still did not attain that beauty she
so much desired; and because of that failure of attain-
ment she would occasionally fall sick, and naught would
cure the sickness save that Frank buy her more bright
stones.

HELEN: Wife of Harvey. Was afflicted with the vice of
lying.

"TRIBUNE" LADY REPORTER: Ardath Williams. A better
newspaperperson than the men she competed with. At
the same time a mother. At the same time a daughter.

A SCULLION MAID: She was for sale. She could be had.

THE WEREWOLF WOMAN: Maggy Szdolny. There was a
curse on her.

FEMALE VOICE RELAYING BEAR-MAN INFORMATION TO JOE:
The possession of Maxine McCourtney: a contralto
voice, throaty, with a hint of adenoids and beer.

THE WITCHES: Hecate, Belre, Demisara, Pamphile, Haut
Roman, Lilith, Alicia, Robinette, Vignoche de la Stew-
art, Salome of Bessarabia, and Perpetua of Galt. The
witch Drusye of the Carpathians, the five sisters of
Nagasaki, the Sybil of Panzoust, the Klawtawnamam
witch of Fettiss Island, Sister Anthony St. Villanova,
Atropis, Mary Cornwall, and the two witches of Skal-
daeniry Forest. Mugissowri, Kate de Brille, and Tlec-
tholeme. Proserpine van Antwerp, Dutch Annie, and
Helen Panacea.

THE SIRENS: Tall, light-haired girls with pale tapering legs and big fruity breasts. Their voices harmonized well together.

GYPSY (UNGRAMMATICAL): Cecily de Brault.

FAT BLONDE: Madame Stradella.

A COUNTRY LASS: Twenty-four years old. Lived out on a chicken ranch. Got up in the morning about the time most dances were breaking up. Milked three cows while Frank Tull was shaving. Had a brother and three younger sisters. Liked picture shows if they were Westerns. Drove a car not very skillfully. Was at her best with a dishtowel. Awfully friendly. After talking with her a little, one always thought what a pity she wasn't a little better-looking. She gave one the impression that whatever one might suggest to her she would be perfectly willing to do. But she was frightfully plain, and one never knew but what she might do a lot of running off at the mouth about it afterwards. Even against those two detriments, however, one of the boys went pretty far with her on a couple of occasions, but he let everything drop when it came to scratch.

ELDERLY LADY: A grandmother. Later a great-grandmother. Like a tree looking at little trees grow up all about it; looking at them proudly, but powerless to help them if they grew warped.

ONE OF THE LORELEI: Her hands and feet and other things were calloused from so much sitting around on the Felsen waiting for mariners to navigate past her on the Rhine. A soprano.

CIRCE: She changed men into swine.

FOOTBOUND CHINESE MAIDENS: Unquestionably it improved their walking; that is, it improved the æsthetics of their walking. It gave them a lilting, stiltlike walk, not designed for long distance, not designed for utility, but designed only to please the eyes of their masters. The deformation fell into critical disrepute when the daughters of the poor adopted it, the daughters who had to work instead of charm.

FRANK TULL'S STENOGRAPHER: A commercial college graduate of the ovarian type.

GIRL FORMERLY A SHE-GOAT: Time after time these transformations are decried in the Old Testament. Today, we live more simply; love less ardently.

VAHINE THAT THE SEA SERPENT ATE: A Polynesian girl. She ate fish and fruit and vegetables. When the sea serpent ate her, she liked it even less than the fish liked it when she ate them.

A FAIR-HAIRED NORDIC GIRL: Elisabeth Poudre.

A GIRL IN APOLLONIUS'S LIFE: A memory.

THE BRIDE OF YOTTLE: Data as to her measurements are lacking. But after the nuptials, after she had left them, after her marriage had been consummated in heaven, the male Woldercanese still thought of her, remembering her beauty. And when they took brides, and kissed them, they made believe it was Yottle's bride they were kissing instead of their own.

THE WOLDERCAN VIRGINS: A dozen green, untasted girls.

III. The Child Characters

SONS OF THE RAILROAD MAN: (a) Ed junior. Barefoot boy with cheeks of tan, except that his cheeks were pale and his mother wouldn't let him go barefoot. (b) Little Howard. Papa spanked him oftener than he did Ed junior.

THE ROGERS CHILDREN: (a) Alice. She stood first in her class all through the public schools but married while still so young that she never amounted to anything. (b) Willie. He operated a filling station after reaching his majority. (c) Little Edna. She died two months after the circus in a traffic accident. She was the prettiest of the Rogers children.

THE LITTLE FAT BROWN BOY: For seven years he was a diner; then for a few minutes he was a dinner. Ultimately he was incorporated into the cell structure of the sea serpent, a distinction he did not enjoy.

ELDERLY LADY'S GRANDSON: Peter R. Roberts. He took his

Ph.D. at Harvard years later. Taught history in a southern school for boys. Married Miss Calanthe Devereau. Achieved the deanship of his department in his fortieth year. Never did he forget Doctor Lao's circus.

LITTLE BOY EVICTED FROM THE CIRCUS GROUNDS BY THE COPS: Gonzalo Pedregon. At nineteen he founded the later-to-be-famous collegiate dance orchestra, "Chalo's Chile Pickers," which through radio broadcasts and movie contracts made a neat bit of change for its director.

LITTLE BOY SLAIN BY THE MAUSER BULLET: A Tongshan kid named Da Go. He would have laughed as readily as the other bystanders had he not been the one who was laughed at.

FROGBOYS: Cretins.

IV. *The Animals*

POLAR BEAR: White like the ice floes among which it wanders. Great Mother Nature—she created snowfields for polar bears and pinewoods for black bears and mountains for grizzly bears and toyshops for teddy bears.

MONKEYS: The little brown brothers. From their cages they stare at us staring at them; then leaning over sniff at clots of their own dung.

HYENA: Africa echoes with its laughter.

SONORAN GRIZZLY: The country cousin living in Mexico of the great family Ursus horribilis.

HERMAPHRODITE GOATS: Resemble fishing worms. Nanny and Billy living together in the same husk.

PONY STALLION: Once in a Middle Western state a show of this sort was going on. The framework broke; the pony stallion fell through and killed the woman. There followed a terrible rumpus. The city aldermen met and argued. Finally, they decided that unless those frameworks were made stronger in the future that sort of show would have to be done away with entirely.

HORSES: Anachronisms less speedy, less beautiful, less efficient than the machines which have replaced them.

GOLDEN ASS: Wolves turn into women, mud into turtles, brown boys into snakes, fish into vahines, goats into girls, men into swine. And Lucius Apuleius, with the aid of Fotis, turned into an ass.

HOUND OF THE HEDGES: A dream.

BURRO: Not a white man's animal.

GILA MONSTERS: Pink and black, clumsy and poisonous, egg-layers, egg-eaters.

BEAST OF THE APOCALYPSE: A legend.

IGUANAS: The nuts from which the dragon stories sprouted.

KIT FOXES: Furry, fugitive, pretty little things.

BADGERS: Hole-diggers.

NAUTILUS: Sometimes chambered. Seabeasts. Speechless, sightless, thoughtless. They sail around on the waves and eat and reproduce and die.

SQUID: Adolescent octopi.

OBELIA: Baby jellies. Medusas. Stingers. Transparent umbrellas.

ELASMOBRANCH SHARKS: Mankillers.

ENORMOUS TURTLES: The tortoises on the Galápagos and Aldabra Islands.

SEA SERPENT'S MATE: She knew what he wanted when she saw him coming through the waves.

SCORPIONS: Very ancient bugs glorified in heaven every night.

CRUSTACEANS: Crawdads. Cornpaffies. You catch them when you are fishing for catfish sometimes. Dangling from your hook they wave their claws and feelers at you, and you wonder at the fantasies that dwell in muddy waters.

LAMBKINS: Food and clothing for the master, man.

COCKROACH: La Cucaracha, the kitchendweller. Decently dressed in brown or black, discreet and humble, he lives in hovels as readily as in grand hotels. He has been with us a long time. He crawled about the middenheaps of the Neanderthal just as he still crawls about the middenheaps of the Parisian. He is fit and he survives. He watched the dinosaur and the pterodactyl die, and he saw Babylon flourish.

SPHINX: The icon of Africa.

STOAT: A stinkpot.

LION: A symbol.

HIPPOPOTAMUS: God must have loved ugly animals, he made so many of them.

CHIMERA: Described by Rabelais, Flaubert, and Finney.

TIGER: Color scheme somewhat the same as that of an Arizona Gila monster. Life cycle somewhat different.

WEREWOLF: Not the American lobo. Probably some species from the Carpathians or Urals.

MINKS: Fierce and beautiful hunters who, when they ease up on their vigilance, find themselves converted into coats and collars.

CATS: They are wild in the heart of the city, but they are tame and frightened in the heart of the woods. They don't fit anywhere any more.

RATTLESNAKES: Killed on sight, hunted and stamped down, they won't last much longer. Probably they wish along with the Aztec Indians that Columbus's boats had all sunk in the middle of the Atlantic.

TANTILLAS: Sonoran tantillas. They have small eyes, but rather large rostrals. Atop their heads they bear a pair of internasals, a pair of prefrontals, a frontal, a supraocular on each side and a pair of parietals. Furthermore, the posterior nasal is in contact with the preocular; and, it is alleged, their anterior genials are longer than their posterior genials.

SPOTTED NIGHT SNAKES: Hypsiglena ochrorhynchus ochrorhynchus. A very small snake. A very pretty snake. A very secretive snake. Mother Nature has provided for its diet very small, very pretty, and very secretive lizards. So down among the grasses of the irrigated fields the secretive, pretty little snakes chase and catch and eat the secretive, pretty little lizards. And the lizards which do not get caught breed and reproduce more pretty little lizards so that the oncoming generations of Hypsiglena may have plenty to eat. Furthermore, the little lizards eat little bugs, which in turn eat littler bugs, themselves eating vegetation of a sort which has reared its flowers among the decay of animal flesh; and round and round and roundabout the merry dance of eating goes on till each little live thing knows not whether he was designed to be the diner or the dinner.

FADED SNAKES: Lizard-eaters, too; and they also eat each other.

SEA SERPENT: No one has counted his genials and gastroteges yet, nor computed his parietals and described his supraoculars, though there's plenty would like to and pickle him to boot and stick him in a museum for people to peer at.

FRIGATE BIRD: They rove and roam the whole wide ocean with hardly a wing-flap, yet a little canary threshes its wings a thousand times to rise to a perch in a tree.

MERMAID: Described in the text.

SATYR: Described in the text.

ROC: Really not as big as Sinbad thought it was, but plenty big enough to do all that he said it did.

UNICORN: A decorative device on a mustard pot.

MEDUSA: As frigid herself as the stone figures into which she converted men.

WALRUS: Eskimo food.

CAMELS: The daughters of the desert throw sand in their eyes; a curious reaction follows, and the daughters laugh.

BOA: A little snake that squeezes.

ANACONDA: A giant snake that squeezes.

GRASS SNAKE: The one which ornamented the hound of the hedges was of the Coronella group.

GNATS: Mother Nature's tiniest flying machines.

RATS: They fight with cockroaches for the crust left under the table. And once they knew glory: they ate a bishop.

KATYDIDS: Remnants of an Egyptian plague.

BATS: Unsurpassed as small game. The only time one can

hunt them is at dusk when the light is poor and fleeting. It takes a good shot to bring one of them down.

TURTLES (SNAPPING): They like to lie buried in the mud with only their noseholes sticking out. So Nature generously arranged nice sloughs of mud wherever there were any snapping turtles; and there they lie buried with only their noseholes sticking out. Nature always provides things for the comfort of her children.

TURTLE (TWO-HEADED): It died shortly. It could never stop quarreling with itself at feeding time, each head desiring to do all the eating. Once Apollonius, to test its reactions, placed two little lady turtles a few inches away from either head. The thing thereupon nearly tore itself in two.

CRICKETS: Ethiopian grasshoppers.

SALAMANDERS: The little water-lizards, not the water-fairies; though they, too, are interesting. Baby salamanders are gluey white and from their cheeks dangle atrocious-looking gills. Grown-up salamanders are muddy-looking, and as mud puppies are cut up by co-eds in comparative anatomy classes for some purpose never clearly explained. However, it is safe to say that the whole, sole, one and only purpose of salamanders living at all is that in the guise of mud puppies they may be cut into pieces by co-eds in colleges for some purpose never clearly explained. Though it may also be argued that the whole, sole, one and only purpose of co-eds being alive is that in comparative anatomy classes in college they may cut up mud puppies for some reason never clearly explained.

FROGS: The minstrels.

TOADS: Minstrels, too, in their fashion, but not such virtuosi as their more edible relatives.

MINNOWS: Baby fishes on which their aunts and uncles feed.

COLONY OF PARASITES: Lowly life forms. Ciliated and amorphous and equipped with contractile vacuoles.

TICKS: Paradoxes. When they are not feeding on blood,

they are blood-red. When they are feeding on blood, they are grey as soap.

POLAND CHINA SHOAT: Food for man.

DUROC JERSEY PIG: Food for man.

GADARENE SWINE: Food for sermons.

HEDGEHOGS: Quiet little pincushions that hate the rain and are unimpressed by the revolutions among the men whose countrysides they adorn.

ELEPHANTS: Grandchildren of the mastodons.

SIDEWINDERS: They walk sideways as a measuring worm walks longways, although not exactly. On their brows they bear the ancient device of cuckoldry. On their tails is a toy. They are yellow as the sands they prowl about in, and from their fangs a venomous syrup drips.

GEESE: They please something in man's palate and therefore are permitted to live.

JERSEY CATTLE: They survive for the same reason all geese survive.

SNAILS: Make their own roads of slime and enjoy the sensation of travel without going anywhere.

STRAY SONGBIRDS GASPING IN THE HEAT: Six sparrows. One thrush.

MARMOTS: Groundhogs.

FISHING WORMS: Sometimes along with the mud puppies the co-eds cut up fishing worms, too. The fishing worms used in zoology classes are great big fat fellows. There is something pathetic about them, for in order to attain such size a worm has to be slated for dissection. The wild worms never get enough to eat to grow that big.

SURINAM TOAD: A slender-fingered, slender-nosed, poisonous toad that likes to loaf under water. It is poisonous in the same manner that a toadstool is poisonous: you have to bite the toad to be poisoned. Probably the nadir of all poison systems. A confined Surinam toad in an interesting condition is more instructive to observe than a Cæsarian section. The babies pop out of mama's back and go off immediately about their business.

V. The Gods and Goddesses

YOTTLE: An omnipotent, omniscient, omnipresent lump of bronze.

LARES DOMESTICI: The household gods.

PAN: Physically the largest of all the gods. In his troupe were lemures, ægipanes, bassarides, bacchides, evantes, mænades, fauns, and sylvans. They all adored him.

JESUS OF NAZARETH: Born of the Virgin Mary, uffered under Pontius Pilate, was crucified, died nd was buried. But on the third day He rose again from the cead, nd now He sitteth in Heaven on the right hand of Cod the Father Almighty, Maker of Heaven and earth.

BEL-MARDUK: The one to whom the Babylonians prayed.

BALDER: The Adonis of the north.

ADONIS: The Balder of the south.

APHRODITE: The beautiful goddess.

MUMBO JUMBO: Lord of the Congo.

SATAN MEKRATRIG: Our old enemy.

VI. The Cities

TU-JENG: Solid brick. All about it are red brick kilns breathing reddish smoke into the dead air. And the road past Tu-jeng is red for it is made of chips and slivers of brick. And the water in the canal near Tu-jeng is red and runs through red clay banks. But everything is a dead red, not the cool red of wine, nor the hot red cf blood, nor the blood-red of hate.

ABALONE: A desert town founded by the Conquistadores.

ALEXANDRIA: Still glorifies the name of its maker.

TONGSHAN: A Chinese mining town with a railroad station and army barracks.

TIENTSIN: One of the monster cities of the world. Scene of much war. But whenever its buildings are shot down, Tientsin builds bigger and finer ones to replace them.

BEESWAX: A mining town in Arizona.

SEDALIA: A railroad town in the heart of the Missouri farmlands.

PEIPING: Peking. The Northern Capital. Tientsin's huge old sister.

SHANHAIKWAN: The town at the northern end of the Great Wall.

PLACE OF MUD SHACKS AND DARKY PEOPLE: Unidentified.

WOLDERCAN: A hieroglyph on a potsherd.

VII. The Statuettes, Figurines, Icons, Artifacts, and Idols

YOTTLE: Bronze.

KATE: Carnelian chalcedony.

SPHINX: (MRS. ROGERS'S): Terra cotta.

SPHINX: (WINKELMANN'S): Ivory.

SPHINX: (EGYPTIAN): Sandstone.

ONE ANONYMOUS MAN: Sandstone.

ELEVEN ANONYMOUS ONLOOKERS: Chert.

TEN DRUNKEN SAILORS: Chert and schist.

THE BUDDHA: Jade.

CRUCIFIX: Gold.

CHIMERA (ALEXANDRIAN): Rags and clay and hide and bones.

CHIMERA (TIBETAN): Porcelain.

CHIMERA (KUBLAI'S): Bronze.

EPHESIAN DIANA: Rosewood.

LINGAM: Second growth black walnut.

YOTTLE'S SACRED STONE AX: Basalt.

VIII. The Questions and Contradictions and Obscurities

1. Was it a bear or a Russian or what?
2. If the sea serpent was as poisonous as it claimed to be, why didn't it kill the chimera when it bit him?
3. Why, after all the discussion between himself and his wife, didn't Frank Tull hunt up the bear and see what it really was?

4. Why should Apollonius of Tyana, who claimed superiority to Christ, fall back on the crucifix to banish Satan?

5. Why didn't the two college punks get sore when they were thrown out?

6. Why didn't Doctor Lao notice anything unusual when he found Miss Agnes Birdsong and the satyr in such a compromising posture?

7. What was the business that the dead man whom Apollonius resurrected had to attend to?

8. What did Mumbo Jumbo do with the fair-haired Nordic girl?

9. If the circus didn't come to Abalone on the railroad and didn't come on trucks, how did it get there?

10. What happened to the eleven people who were turned to stone when the medusa dropped her blindfold?

11. If Apollonius was such a great magician, why did he waste his time fooling around with a little circus?

12. Inasmuch as legend tells us that chimeras were invariably females, how did it happen that Doctor Lao's was a male?

13. Was it for this same reason that Tu-jeng, when Doctor Lao caught the satyr there, was a hamlet near the Great Wall, whereas it is now a suburb of Tientsin?

IX. The Foodstuffs

Pork chops. Lettuce. Ham hocks. Lamb chops. Persimmons. Hay. Soda pop. Duck eggs. Garlic. Little fat brown boy. Candy. Onion seeds. Pie. Pelicans. Grapes. Proteins. Snails. Beer. Snow geese. Sea foods. Carbohydrates. Frigate bird. Butterfat. Chicken. Gooseliver. Fish. Vahine. Frogs. Bananas. Oysters. Brown boy's old pappy. Bugs. Plantain. Fishing worms. Little plants. Lizards. Grub worms. Hot dogs. Rattlesnakes. Noodles. Slop. Nuts.

Tientsin-Tucson, 1929-1934.

ABOUT THE AUTHOR

*Charles G. Finney, born in Sedalia, Missouri, served
in the 15th Infantry in China, where he wrote this
book. He published an army memoir and three
novels while working at the Arizona Daily Star,
and he lives in Tucson today.*

V-814   **ABE, KOBO** / The Woman in the Dunes
V-2014   **AUDEN, W. H.** / Collected Longer Poems
V-2015   **AUDEN, W. H.** / Collected Shorter Poems 1927-1957
V-102   **AUDEN, W. H.** / Selected Poetry of W. H. Auden
V-601   **AUDEN, W. H. AND PAUL B. TAYLOR (trans.)** / The Elder Edda
V-20   **BABIN, MARIA-THERESA AND STAN STEINER (eds.)** / Borinquen: An Anthology of Puerto-Rican Literature
V-271   **BEDIER, JOSEPH** / Tristan and Iseult
V-523   **BELLAMY, JOE DAVID (ed.)** / Superfiction or The American Story Transformed: An Anthology
V-72   **BERNIKOW, LOUISE (ed.)** / The World Split Open: Four Centuries of Women Poets in England and America 1552-1950
V-321   **BOLT, ROBERT** / A Man for All Seasons
V-21   **BOWEN, ELIZABETH** / The Death of the Heart
V-294   **BRADBURY, RAY** / The Vintage Bradbury
V-670   **BRECHT, BERTOLT (ed. by Ralph Manheim and John Willett)** / Collected Plays, Vol. 1
V-759   **BRECHT, BERTOLT (ed. by Ralph Manheim and John Willett)** / Collected Plays, Vol. 5
V-216   **BRECHT, BERTOLT (ed. by Ralph Manheim and John Willett)** / Collected Plays, Vol. 7
V-819   **BRECHT, BERTOLT (ed. by Ralph Manheim and John Willett)** / Collected Plays, Vol. 9
V-841   **BYNNER, WITTER AND KIANG KANG-HU (eds.)** / The Jade Mountain: A Chinese Anthology
V-207   **CAMUS, ALBERT** / Caligula & Three Other Plays
V-281   **CAMUS, ALBERT** / Exile and the Kingdom
V-223   **CAMUS, ALBERT** / The Fall
V-865   **CAMUS, ALBERT** / A Happy Death: A Novel
V-626   **CAMUS, ALBERT** / Lyrical and Critical Essays
V-75   **CAMUS, ALBERT** / The Myth of Sisyphus and Other Essays
V-258   **CAMUS, ALBERT** / The Plague
V-245   **CAMUS, ALBERT** / The Possessed
V-30   **CAMUS, ALBERT** / The Rebel
V-2   **CAMUS, ALBERT** / The Stranger
V-28   **CATHER, WILLA** / Five Stories
V-705   **CATHER, WILLA** / A Lost Lady
V-200   **CATHER, WILLA** / My Mortal Enemy
V-179   **CATHER, WILLA** / Obscure Destinies
V-252   **CATHER, WILLA** / One of Ours
V-913   **CATHER, WILLA** / The Professor's House
V-434   **CATHER, WILLA** / Sapphira and the Slave Girl
V-680   **CATHER, WILLA** / Shadows on the Rock
V-684   **CATHER, WILLA** / Youth and the Bright Medusa
V-140   **CERF, BENNETT (ed.)** / Famous Ghost Stories
V-203   **CERF, BENNETT (ed.)** / Four Contemporary American Plays
V-127   **CERF, BENNETT (ed.)** / Great Modern Short Stories
V-326   **CERF, CHRISTOPHER (ed.)** / The Vintage Anthology of Science Fantasy
V-293   **CHAUCER, GEOFFREY** / The Canterbury Tales (a prose version in Modern English)
V-142   **CHAUCER, GEOFFREY** / Troilus and Cressida
V-723   **CHERNYSHEVSKY, N. G.** / What Is to Be Done?
V-173   **CONFUCIUS (trans. by Arthur Waley)** / Analects
V-155   **CONRAD, JOSEPH** / Three Great Tales: The Nigger of the Narcissus, Heart of Darkness, Youth
V-10   **CRANE, STEPHEN** / Stories and Tales
V-126   **DANTE, ALIGHIERI** / The Divine Comedy
V-177   **DINESEN, ISAK** / Anecdotes of Destiny